VISIONS FROM THE VOID

12 TALES INSPIRED BY 12 TWISTED DESIGNS

ADAM MILLARD
LYDIAN FAUST
KIT POWER
DUNCAN P. BRADSHAW
PAULA D. ASHE
AND MORE...

COMPILED BY JONATHAN BUTCHER ARTWORK BY LES BUTCHER

Copyright Matthew Cash Burdizzo Books 2018

Edited by Matthew Cash, Burdizzo Books

All rights reserved. No part of this book may be reproduced in any form or by any means, except by inclusion of brief quotations in a review, without permission in writing from the publisher. Each author retains copyright of their own individual story.

This book is a work of fiction. The characters and situations in this book are imaginary. No resemblance is intended between these characters and any persons, living, dead, or undead.

This book is sold subject to the condition that it shall not, by way of trade or otherwise, be lent, resold, hired out or otherwise circulated without the publisher's prior consent in any form or binding or cover other than that in which it is published and without similar condition including this condition being imposed on the subsequent purchaser

Published in Great Britain in 2018 by Matthew Cash, Burdizzo Books Walsall, UK

Contents

Introduction 5

Kayleigh Marie Edwards – Shut Up and Dance 7

Adam Millard – Checkmate 31

Emma Dehaney – Ten-Minute Warning 51

John McNee – Uncommon Time 61

Paula D. Ashe – Exile in Extremis 87

Kit Power – The Prickles 119

Jonathan Butcher – The Jazziverse 131

Lydian Faust – Third-Eye 161

David Court – Brother, Can You Spare a Paradigm? 179

J. G. Clay – The Cruellest Gift 197

Duncan P. Bradshaw – It Sucks When You're All Seeds and No Feathers 229

Matthew Cash – Grotto 253

The Authors 279

Welcome...

For as long as I can remember, I've known my dad as an artist.

As a younger man, Les Butcher painted black-and-white op-art designs, and I was glad that as a retired man he rediscovered his creative roots. The jagged, mesmerising, and often violent nature of his designs always captivated me. There's something striking and often disorientating about even his simpler pieces, and I love them for their surreal artistry.

Dad has never promoted his pictures, attempted to push them to a wider audience, or tried to sell them. The designs you will see in this collection have, until now, been seen by no more than a dozen or so people, so I'm proud to unleash them here.

Having become acquainted with some incredible writers over the last couple of years, a while ago I started to wonder whether these designs could inspire stories, and if they could, what the hell kind of tales would they be?

I hope you enjoy finding out.

Jonathan Butcher, 15/5/2018

Shut Up And Dance

Kayleigh Marie Edwards

Alison Morris had always found the suggestion to 'try to enjoy' oneself peculiar; she thought that if you had to try then you really weren't having a good time. Alison used to enjoy going to festivals, but now that she was in her thirties, it had been quite some time since she had spent a weekend in muddy boots with no access to a hot (or cold) shower. She would have struggled to get past sleeping in a bag on the ground for a festival she actually liked, but this pop-punk *Free* festival was her idea of hell. She hated the music, hated the abundance of hallucinogenic drugs, and hated having to stand outside in a downpour. Mostly, she hated that she was so grumpy but that was who she was. Her idea of being free was being able to stay inside with the curtains shut.

The only reason that she was currently standing in a crowd of leather jackets and sewn-on band patches was because Meg, her sister, had bought the ticket for her. Of course, she had expressed no desire to attend *Free*, but Meg wasn't having any of it. The moment that Alison had objected, she was hit with a guilt trip about how Meg had spent what little money she had on trying to plan something fun for them. Within a minute, she'd been made to feel like the most ungrateful person on the planet and then she'd been talked into 'giving it a go'. Now that she was rain-soaked and freezing, she wished she had stuck to her guns.

Meg was one of those people who appeared to have a heart of gold. Meg was always the first to point out that she'd do anything for anyone. She was a *kind* person. To anyone else, she looked like she'd just gone out of her way to treat her sister. But Alison knew her better. Meg never did anything nice because nothing ever came without an ulterior motive. In this case, Alison suspected that Meg simply couldn't find anyone else to go to *Free* with. She'd been dragged to several events in the past that were of absolutely no interest to her, just so that Meg had company.

The longer Alison stood in the rain, enduring what she considered to be obsessive double kicking from the drummer onstage, the more irritated she felt. At first, she was merely annoyed by Meg's lack of consideration for her long-standing and vehement hatred of pop-punk. She knew that Meg couldn't care less whether they both had a good time, so long as Meg had a good time. But as the hours had passed, the ridiculous notion that Meg had brought her here specifically to spite her was gaining traction.

When they were kids, they had shared a room. Meg had become obsessed with one annoying, chirpy CD, and had played it over and over until Alison detested the entire music sub-genre and every band in it. In retaliation, Alison had tried to drown it out with a heavy metal CD on repeat. As a result, both girls had grown up with an equally exaggerated hatred of each other's tastes in almost everything. The longer Alison reflected on her most annoying memories of Meg, the more convinced she was that she had been dragged here as some sort of payback for Meg's forced introduction to Machine head.

She was snapped out of her thoughts by Meg's flailing arms smacking her in the head. She looked at her oblivious sister, who was thrashing around as though bees were attacking her. Meg was having the time of her life, and it annoyed Alison to no end.

Returning to reality and the present, Alison looked around. It seemed that everyone around her was being attacked by bees or trying to stamp out small fires. People were headbanging. Guitars were wailing, but only in three chords. The sun had gone down hours ago and the field was lit by gigantic spotlights that seemed to be there just to give her a headache. The festival site itself was in the Oxfordshire countryside, one of the most beautiful places that Alison had ever seen. The main stage arena was in a huge field. To her right, a small path led to the second arena, and to her left lay the woods, which were fenced off. As a fan of nature, she knew that she should have at least been able to appreciate where she was, but she just couldn't. Any peaceful thought she had was overshadowed by the sincere concern that she was going to wake up to find Meg choking on drug-induced vomit. Alison had never taken drugs herself, and as a result she had the naive, paranoid fear that comes with the unshakeable, though misguided and exaggerated, knowledge that taking drugs – any drugs – inevitably leads to death. It didn't take a genius to spot that half the crowd were on something.

She crossed her arms and wondered how long she was going to have to stand there in the mud before Meg let her return to their leaking tent. That was when she heard it. Amidst the uniformed chaos, the sound was so out of place that it was jarring, and what was even stranger was that no one else reacted to it. For just a moment, Alison was absolutely positive that she'd heard a saxophone.

Something lukewarm splashed over her arm as a twenty-something-year-old man fell into her. She glared at him, realising he'd spilled an entire plastic cup of beer on her. He didn't even seem to notice. He grinned at her, made the devil horns sign with both hands, and cried, "Hardcore!" She didn't really know what that meant. Before she had decided whether or not she could be bothered to elicit a response, she heard a bass drum completely unlike the one on stage. What she heard actually had *rhythm*. She looked around, searching for the source. There was something else going on at this stupid festival, something that had actually piqued her interest, and she wanted to find it. There was so much going on around her, and everything was so loud, that she didn't even know which direction it was coming from at first. But then she looked towards the woods and saw something impossible.

Black light.

It hung over the woods, not like a cloud, but a shield. It pulsed in time with the smooth sounds that came from within. She blinked, knowing that such a thing as black light – especially at night - just couldn't be. And yet it was. She wanted to be inside it.

Unaware that she was moving, she headed for the woods.

Meg's cold hand reached into the dark and grabbed Alison's arm. The squeezing sensation on her flesh snapped Alison out of her trance, but not completely. Dizzy, she turned to look at her sister, who was staring at her as though she'd lost her mind. Behind them was the perimeter fence, which Alison didn't have so much as a vague recollection of climbing over. She tried to remember leaving the crowd, but she couldn't. All she knew was the desire to find the source of the black light and crawl into the darkness. Behind them, the festival and all its lights and sounds and atmosphere continued, but they were no longer a part of it. They were a lot further away from everything than either of them could have realised.

"Dude, where the hell are you going?" Meg asked, with a complete lack of genuine curiosity but a lot of annoyance.

"I just want to see what's in there," Alison replied. She was quiet, distant, but Meg was too self-involved to notice. Alison looked through the thick branches. That smooth music was louder now. Closer. Meg followed her gaze, wrongly but understandably assuming that the woods were what Alison meant by 'in there'.

Meg stared into the trees, trying to understand what the fascination was, and then grew bored. She turned to Alison, more annoyed than ever that she was missing out on her favourite band, Ballsack.

"Well…those are trees. You fucking psycho." Meg tugged on Alison's arm, trying to pull her back towards the fence. Alison ignored her and took off into the woods and out of the illumination of the furthest reaching lights from the main arena. Unwilling to let go of her sister's arm, Meg was dragged along with her. She protested but Alison couldn't even hear her anymore.

Soon, they were in complete darkness and Meg had no idea how Alison seemed to know exactly where they were going. Alison was following the music of course, but Meg didn't know that because she couldn't hear it. All Meg could hear was the sound of the rain pelting the canopy of branches above them. Meg probably would have been panicking had she been there with anyone else, but Alison had always been so sensible. Boring, even. There was no way she'd lead them into anything remotely exciting, let alone dangerous, Meg thought. Her sister was not the most relaxed person, but she was the most trustworthy.

They pushed through one last thick cluster of trees and came out in a huge clearing. The space was filled with an enormous, white tent. Meg thought it looked like a circus tent, only without all the jolly colours. Alison stopped in her tracks, feeling warm. The black light surrounded the tent, encapsulated it. Music soared from inside; brass, wind, and strings all at once. Alison had never found anything so inviting in all her life. Meg finally let go of Alison's arm and rushed towards it, excited.

"Al, how did you know about this? Where were the clues?" Meg squealed. She couldn't stand still; she was dying to go inside and didn't understand why Alison had just stopped. Meg had been to many a festival in her time, a few of which had 'secret events' that could normally be discovered by solving clues on the website, or hints at the festival itself. The secret was normally just an unannounced band or artist, so this was something special. She'd never seen anything quite this hidden or elaborate.

They found a gap in the curtain and entered.

The moment that the girls stepped inside, they forgot that they were in a tent.

The party was in full swing. A huge bar lined one side, and a stage that housed a full swing band, complete with a trio of female singers, lined the other. Above the band hung a white banner that read 'The Swing Demons'. Chairs and tables were spread out around the edges of a vast dance floor, which was full. Couples were twirling and throwing and catching their partners. The air was full of laughter. Neither sister had ever experienced an atmosphere so lively.

Almost everyone was dressed up. Meg cursed herself for not finding the clues that these people must have uncovered, because judging by their outfits, they had all turned up to *Free* prepared for this event. The men were all in various types of formal wear; some wore suits, others wore shirts and braces, all wore shined shoes. Several wore hats, and several even had coat tails on their jackets.

The women were like a pin-up line-up from across the decades. Some wore knee-length shift dresses adorned with tassels and headbands and feathers and pearl necklaces. Others wore full skirts, corsets, and satin gloves. Meg had never seen so many hair fascinators and twirling petticoats.

Even the musicians were dressed differently – all formal, but all looked like they were from a different decade – not even the singers matched each other.

The only exceptions were a group of four young adults, dressed casually, sat at a table on the edge of the dance floor. All of them cradled drinks in their hands, all of them looked nervous, and all of them were staring at Alison and Meg. Alison stared back, noticing that their expressions much resembled what hers probably looked like only half an hour before.

And the music – oh! The music! To Alison and Meg, it simultaneously sounded like nothing they'd ever heard, and everything they'd ever heard altogether. They'd both heard jazz and swing music before, but not like this. Nothing like this. It was a blend of the very best of everything from the last hundred years or so. Every time they thought they recognised something, it changed into something else.

A handsome man in a black flat cap approached and asked Meg to dance. She grinned and took his hand, about to waltz off to the dance floor, when she was snatched backwards. This time, it was her arm that was being squeezed too tightly by her sister. Alison was holding on to Meg so hard that the skin of her arm had gone white underneath her fingers, and Alison was glaring at the handsome man, who had not released Meg's hand yet.

"Al, what the hell?" Meg growled, through gritted teeth. She just didn't get her sister. It was only minutes ago that Alison had wandered off into the woods like a lunatic, taking them away from the main festival site and bringing them here. But now she was suddenly acting suspicious. Meg fought the urge to slap the boring out of her.

"Let go of my sister," Alison said, staring the man in the eyes. The smile stayed on his lips, but his eyes revealed something else that Alison recognised and didn't like. *Fear.*

"It's a party, you gotta dance!" He grinned, looking from Alison to Meg and then back to Alison. Meg tried to tug her arm out of Alison's grasp but failed. The man took a step closer. He was still smiling but Alison could see how much of a strain it was for him. "It's a party," he said again, and then quietly, "he doesn't like it if we're not having fun. It's the rules." With that, he pulled Meg away from Alison and they disappeared on to the dance floor. Alison stared after them, horrified. Who the hell was 'he'?

She stood there for what felt like a long time, watching Meg on the dance floor and cursing herself for not snapping out of whatever haze she'd been in until it was too late. That alluring black light and the music had drawn her away from the festival. It had been so inviting, so promising. The closer she'd got to it, the safer she'd felt. It was as though she'd been heading to a home she never knew she had. Now, as she stood amidst this spectacular party, she knew she'd been tricked. Meg, ever looking inward, couldn't see it. But Alison could. She could hear the laughter, but she could also hear what was underneath it. Strained voices, sore throats, *raw* throats. The laughter was forced, painful. She saw the smiles on everyone's faces, no, the *grins*. Wide, toothy grins. The kind you make when you're a kid and you're having a photo taken and someone has instructed you to say cheese. She saw those grins. But she also saw the twitching muscles that were holding them up, a sea of exhausted faces whose eyes didn't match their mouths. It was the eyes that were most telling. Eyes half-closed, tired. Eyes that were streaming with tears. Eyes that were not laughing, but screaming.

She thought of the pull of that black light again, and felt a fool. She fancied herself a moth that had just flown into an open flame. And worse, she had just dragged her sister in with her.

She felt for the gap in the curtains that they had entered through, and was unsurprised that it now somehow ceased to exist. She looked around for another exit, but knew that there were none.

Like everyone else at this spectacular party, she was frozen. She was the kind of person to always have a plan and a way out of anything, but from the moment she had heard that first note, she'd been out of her own control. Her only comfort was that she knew she wouldn't lose her sister, not even in this crowd. Meg, try as she might to blend in, stuck out like a sore thumb on the dance floor. She just didn't know the steps and couldn't keep in time. Everyone else looked like they'd been dancing there together for years. The thought made her feel cold.

Twenty minutes later, perched on a stool at the bar, Alison was contemplating ordering a drink, a *real* drink. She never touched alcohol anymore, but if ever there was a time to try and dull the senses, it was now. She'd already circled the crowd, feeling along every inch of the tent for an opening. She'd even tried to crawl underneath it, but all she'd found when she lifted one curtain was layers and layers of more material. She'd stopped when she'd realised that a lot of people were starting to stare at her, afraid. Initially, she thought they were afraid of her, but then it occurred to her that they were afraid *for* her. So she'd taken a seat at the bar and stayed still for a while. She didn't know why but she suspected that being the centre of attention was not a good idea in this place.

Every now and then, she looked over her shoulder to make sure that Meg was still there on the dance floor. The man who danced with her had seemed like a threat at first, and now Alison knew different. She had become quite certain that he was just trying to help them, to get them to blend in with everyone else. Blending in, for some reason, felt crucial here.

The only other people who had her attention were the group of casual, frowning, young adults. She'd noticed how out of place they were. She'd also noticed that a lot of people were looking at them too.

She decided to get that drink, and looked for the bartender, who was mixing a cocktail. He was dressed in a white shirt and a waistcoat. On first glance, he was perfectly neat. On second glance, his shirt was stained and soaked with sweat. He had a white towel slung over his shoulder, and it was splattered with blood. He moved slowly, and with a limp.

To Alison's right, a woman in a glamorous red dress perched on a stool. She smoked a crisp, white cigarette through a silver cigarette holder. Every time she drew in a breath, her eyes watered and her chest heaved with a silent cough. Her otherwise perfectly applied makeup was streaked with old, dried tears. And yet, she continued to smoke. And grin.

Alison got the bartender's attention and ordered 'whatever'. She was presented with a gin martini, complete with a green olive. She took it and turned on her stool, leaning back against the bar. Being made of solid wood, it took her weight easily, which Alison thought was strange for a pop-up bar in a pop-up marquee. She faced the stage and watched the musicians. Several of them had bleeding fingers. The worst was the double-bassist, who had narrow rivers of blood running from his hands and down his bass. And yet, they all grinned.

A man in a white shirt tap-danced on the dance floor. People around him clapped and cheered as his feet moved in perfect time. He appeared to be happy, but underneath his grin was that same strain that everyone else wore. For a moment, she thought she heard him screaming.

The music took on a new tone, sounding off. The singer's voices no longer complemented each other in harmony, but grated against each other. Wrong notes were hit. A string snapped. But no one stopped. The music's tempo slid from upbeat to chaotic, and that, mixed with the screams that she'd first thought were laughter, filled her head. She felt like she was going mad. Her only anchor to reality, and a reminder that this *couldn't be* reality, was Meg.

"…with me." The voice was quiet and weak, and barely caught Alison's attention. She took her eyes off Meg and looked at the guy in the black sweater. He wasn't smiling like the others, and she recognised him from the table at the edge of the dance floor. "Come with me," he repeated. He slid an arm around her waist and pulled her down from the barstool. She spilled her martini but didn't notice, and followed him back to his table, where she sat down. Three pairs of terrified eyes stared at her, but none of them said anything. She looked to the one who had approached her and gestured for him to start talking.

"Do you know how to get out?" He looked sincere but Alison burst into laughter. She didn't find his question humorous, but infuriating. Why would she know a way out? She knew that he'd watched her all around the room, failing to escape, and so his question was ridiculous. When she was done with her outburst, she looked at their scared faces, from one to the other. They looked terrified. The girl closest to her was staring straight ahead with a determination in her eyes that said, *no, not me*. But the corners of her mouth kept twitching, as though her mouth was trying to pull itself upwards into a smile against her will.

"We were camping," the guy in the black sweater explained. "Dave kept going on about this music and ran off, so we followed him. None of us knew what he was talking about, we just thought he was drunk. And then we found this place."

"And we've been here ever since," his friend finished. His voice was barely a whisper.

"I heard the music too," Alison replied. "Dave, did you see the black light?"

"I'm not Dave," he replied, so angry that he was barely able to spit the words out. The guy in the black sweater put an arm around his friend.

"So where is this Dave now?" Alison pressed. The four of them looked at each other and then the girl who was trying not to grin started to cry.

"He left us here," the man who wasn't Dave replied. "Don't even know when anymore. Days. Months? We lost track."

"But how did he get out?" Alison continued, now hopeful. None of them replied. The girl who had said nothing so far just shook her head and looked at the black sweater guy with eyes that pleaded with him to keep his mouth shut. A waitress in a sparkly outfit arrived at the table – grinning, of course – and put five shots of a gold liquid in front of them. The four strangers immediately threw them back, all of them wincing at the aftertaste. Alison pushed hers away.

"You have to drink," the mute girl suddenly spoke up. "It's the rules."

...he doesn't like it if we're not having fun. It's the rules.

That's the second time I've heard that, Alison thought. Black Sweater Guy looked around, and then leaned towards her.

"Listen, we haven't been here as long as everyone else so we're not like them yet. There's got to be a way out, right? If we just put our heads together, then…"

"James, stop it," the girl, who was now smiling despite herself, hissed. James ignored her and looked at Alison.

"They're all too scared to do anything, but I'm not. And I don't think you are either."

"James, we're not allowed to talk about leaving," the smiling girl whispered. *'It's the rules'* Alison thought. The smiling girl was crying now, panicked. Sweat glued her fringe to her forehead. She was looking at Alison like she was going to be the undoing of all of them.

"Please, you have to help us…" James said. As the last word left his mouth, James burst into flames. The mute girl screamed and then slapped her hands to her mouth. The guy who wasn't Dave skidded back in his chair to avoid being engulfed. The smiling/crying girl averted her eyes and made not a sound, but her face scrunched up and she cried.

Alison jumped out of her seat and backed up onto the edge of the dance floor.

The music faltered, but only for a second, and then it continued. A couple of people on the dance floor lost their footing, but just for a moment. Alison, rubbing her singed arms, had the terrible thought that they'd all seen something like this before. The only other person who reacted to a man going up in flames was Meg. She was frozen where she stood with wide eyes and her hands pressed to her mouth.

James screamed and burned and the sound was so terrible that Alison would have given anything for it to stop.

The bartender approached them, his grin even wider, more strained, than it had been before. He limped on swollen feet, slightly hunched over as though he'd been stood for so long that his back could no longer keep him completely upright. Then, before Alison's eyes, his posture changed and he swaggered towards her. He continued to grin, but it no longer looked like an effort. The bartender was still in there somewhere, but someone or something else had just taken hold of his reigns.

He side-stepped James, who was on the floor and still screaming, stopped in front of Alison, put his hands in his pockets, and leaned back on his heels. His eyes, which had been normal before, were now just black. They pulsed, as though something lived within them. The black light.

"The morrrrre, the merrrriiier," he said. The words were unnatural from his lips, like he was just trying them on for size but they didn't quite fit. "Do you wishhh to stttay, or wishhh to leave?"

Alison paused, surprised. He sounded like he was sincerely giving her the option. But it was surely a trick, and she didn't know how to answer.

"We want to leave," Meg said, from behind her. His head turned in her direction so fast that Alison heard his neck snap. His eyes somehow grew darker.

"Yoooou don't deccccide," he hissed, in several voices. His head snapped back to look at Alison. "You decccide."

Because the black light brought me here. Me, Alison thought. It had called to her; she was the one who had responded to it.

James was whimpering now. Alison looked at him and saw how much pain he was in. He should have been dead. She wondered if anyone here even *could* die. The bartender extended his hands and shrugged, twisting his wrists just a bit too far, in a gesture that asked for her answer.

"Can we please leave?"

He laughed. Behind her, the band still played, and people still danced. He shook one finger from side to side, *no*, like a pendulum swinging.

"Not wwwweeeee. Jusssst one. You deccccide."

Alison closed her eyes, realising that that's what was meant when she was told that Dave had left them here. It had been him who had led them to the party, and it was he who decided which one of them could leave, and he had decided to save himself. He'd left his friends, forever. He'd doomed them to an eternity of whatever this hell was.

Meg was quiet behind Alison, waiting. Trusting. It was unlike her to be silent, but silent she was. Alison looked into his black eyes, and they pulsed. The bartender clapped, suddenly full of glee.

"As you wissssh," he said, and the gap that Alison and Meg had entered through reappeared and opened up. Several people noticed, but none dared to approach it.

"But I didn't…" Alison protested, trembling. He laughed.

"Yessssss, you did." He tapped the side of his head with one finger. "I heard yoooou."

Tears fell from Alison's eyes. She turned to Meg, who was either unaware or unaccepting of the fact that she'd just been condemned by her own sister. Alison hung her head and headed towards the exit. Meg's expression changed as it hit her.

"Al! No! Don't leave me!" Meg cried, her last word broken by the kind of sob that Alison hadn't heard since they were kids. Alison's heart broke, but she couldn't look back again. She was too ashamed. It was only when she reached the exit that she realised that there was no coming back; if she left now, she would never see her sister again. Meg would be trapped here, along with all the other poor souls who were trapped here, forever.

Her hands shook, but she turned around and looked at the bartender. She didn't need to voice her protest because he heard it, plucked straight from her head. He was enraged before she could get the first word out.

"Yooou chose!" he yelled. The music faltered once more, but then continued. "You gggggo! Or thisssss!"

Alison felt a searing heat in the pit of her stomach and crumpled to the ground as her insides threatened to ignite. The pain was incomparable to anything she could have imagined. She looked at James, who lay at the bartender's feet, burned black, alive and in agony. She screamed as the heat travelled through her body, searing every nerve. It was painful. It was just too much.

She didn't look at Meg.

She just crawled outside.

Kayleigh's Afterword

"I stared at my piece of optical art for quite a long time and what I saw in it was the sun (the white centre with white rays, is what I was seeing). After a while, I started to see the black lines as the sun rays instead, and then wondered what a black sun would look like. I quickly dismissed that idea, but I was really hooked on the idea of black light. Something like that would be so unnatural and spooky, and of course, impossible. The story came to me then."

CHECKMATE

ADAM MILLARD

"I think we should get a divorce."

There was something about the way in which she said it — rehearsed and indifferent, as if she had known all along we would be having this conversation — that made me feel about an inch tall. I stopped buttering George's pancakes and turned to her.

"A divorce?" I said, the word tasting bitter on my tongue. Such a simple little word of two syllables, and yet with so many connotations, so much upheaval and change. Change which I was neither prepared for nor wanted.

Laura sighed, leaned against the kitchen worktop and folded her arms across her chest. I noticed the ring had already been removed from her finger, and it was then that I realised I was still holding the butter knife in my hand, my white-knuckled fingers gripping onto it as George chuntered on at the kitchen table — something about spacemen and rockets — as he awaited his breakfast.

"It's not like you're ever *here*," Laura said, her voice not much more than a whisper. I could see she was trying to keep this little tête-à-tête from our son, who would soon, it would seem, be without a steady father-figure. "You're *obsessed*, Jack. Obsessed with Dante, with bringing him down, but you know what, Jack? I've had enough. I don't want George growing up wondering why his father was too busy leaping back and forth through time to be there — "

"I'm here right now," I said. "And we're getting close, Laura. I can feel it. Dante almost slipped up in 2036—"

"Of course he *almost*," Laura said, no longer able to control her rage. "He *almost* slipped up in 2091, *almost* left some evidence in 1742, *almost* got caught red-handed in 2151, and you were there, one step behind him, because that's where he likes you to be, and what you don't seem to be able to understand is that George and I were here the whole time… here in 2030, wondering whether today is the day we get the holocall from Larsen saying that you're not coming home, that Dante finally turned the tables and finished you off."

"That's not going to happen," I told her, moving closer, reaching out a hand and placing it on her arm. She shook me off and took a step back; I decided not to force the issue. "Look, Dante and me, we have a history. If he wanted me dead, he would have killed me a long time ago. He's had opportunities before—"

"It's a fucking game, Jack," Laura said through gritted teeth. "It's game, and there will be only one winner." She looked across to George, who had taken to crashing cutlery together. When she looked back to me, her eyes were filled with tears, and I knew then that I was wasting my time, that we were getting a divorce, and no amount of pleading was going to change that. "Just be there for George," she said. "After we're done, just be there for him."

A shrill beeping interrupted us. From the kitchen table, George excitedly sang, "Uncle Larsen! Uncle Larsen!" for the beeping meant that I was receiving an incoming holocall from my boss, Wolfgang Larsen, who was not George's uncle, despite my son's thrilled proclamations.

Laura shook her head, but she knew I had to take the call. How could I not? "You know I have—"

"Take the goddamn call," she said, pushing past me to get to George's pancakes, which she carried across the room and unceremoniously deposited in front of our son. He didn't seem to mind, and got stuck right in.

As Laura left the room in a huff, I said, "Accept," and then Larsen was standing in our kitchen alongside me, not quite real but real enough by today's technology.

"Catch you at a bad time?" Larsen asked.

"Not *at* a bad time," I said. "Maybe *in* a bad time." I licked the butter from my fingers and poured myself a bitter coffee.

"Your day just got a helluva lot worse, Jack," Larsen said. "Or a helluva lot better, depending on how it pans out—"

"What is it, Larsen?" The anticipation was killing me. At this rate, it would succeed before the bitter coffee did.

"Well, you're not gonna believe this, but Dante just showed up at the Brooklyn Heights Promenade."

The cup slipped from my hand, shattered on the kitchen tiles, sending black-brown liquid spraying out in all directions. "What year?" I said, even though I wasn't sure I could withstand another jump so soon, whether my body would be able to handle the punishment, but I was willing to give it a try if it meant catching Dante. "What year, Larsen?"

"That's the thing, Jack," my superior said as he sucked nervously on a C-Tab, a habit that would kill him before he turned sixty, if he didn't cut down soon. "Dante is here and now, in *this* time."

At first I thought my ears had deceived me, but the grave expression on Larsen's face told me I had heard just fine.

"Not only that, Jack," Larsen went on, "but we have him surrounded. He's not going anywhere, or *anywhen*, but he's refusing to comply until you arrive."

"He asked for me by name?"

Larsen sighed. "Name, badge number, shoe size. It would seem you've made quite the impression across the years."

"No shit."

"We'll hold him until you get here, but you won't believe this, Jack. The fucker's sitting at one of those chess tables. You know? The ones the old timers play at for hours on end?"

I knew what he was talking about. There were a dozen tables with chessboards attached running along one side of the promenade. Right there in the fucking open, as brazen as you like.

"I think he wants to play a game." With that, Larsen terminated the holocall, and once again there was just George and I in the kitchen. George was looking at me with no small amount of suspicion, his face smeared with butter and pancake residue. I wanted to grab him and hug him and tell him that daddy was coming home tonight, that a very bad man was about to go to Cryo for a very long time, but I couldn't. Besides, George wouldn't understand.

"Daddy has to go take care of something," I told my son, whose expression was suddenly filled with confusion. "You understand, don't you?"

George nodded, though I'm not sure he *did* understand. "You betcha!" he said, which made me smile. It was one of his favourite catchphrases, alongside 'okeedokeedoo!', and no matter how many times I heard either, it melted my heart.

"I love you, George."

"Okeedokeedoo!" George said, which was his way of telling me that, no matter what, he would always love me right on back.

I was already reaching for my CPX-250 — not that I wanted Dante dead, but something about this just didn't sit right with me — when Laura came back in the room. Her eyes were red raw, as if she had been crying, and her body language told me she wanted me out of the house, and it was up to me whether I decided to come back or not. "Don't tell me," she said. "Dante."

I didn't even answer, just gathered my stuff and left.

Today's collar would go down in history as one of the most significant in recent years. Centuries, even. Today would be the day that Dante—that sick sonofabitch butcher of more than three-hundred men, women, and children across five centuries either side of me—was brought to justice.

It was a thirty-minute drive to Brooklyn Park Promenade.

I did it in twelve.

The park was filled with unsuspecting citizens. They electrocycled, they jogged with their holographic personal trainers, they kicked balls around the arena, and I wondered whether they would continue to do so if they were aware that, not a couple of hundred feet away, one of the world's most prolific serial killers sat waiting.

Waiting for me.

At one side of the promenade, Larsen and a team of agents stood watch. I had known my superior most of my adult life, trusted no one more—not even my wife—but I had never seen him looking so anxious. In that moment, it was difficult to tell which of us was more nervous, and I was the one Dante had summoned.

"Can you believe this fuck?" Larsen said as I approached from the east. "All he needs is a jam sandwich and a slice of cake, and the sonofabitch might as well be having a picnic."

"He hasn't moved?" I asked, slightly breathless.

"Not one inch," Larsen said. "Just keeps lining those chess pieces up. I swear to Christ we should just put a bullet in him."

I shook my head. That was the last thing we should do. Dante had something up his sleeve; Dante *always* had something up his sleeve. He hadn't evaded capture this long without exits, without ulterior motives and plan B's. I had to give the sick bastard credit: he was good at being a sick bastard.

"Tell your men to stand down," I said, wiping sweat from my brow, even though it was a chill 12 degrees. "I don't want anyone taking him out until I know for sure people aren't in danger."

Larsen knew what I was talking about. Dante made a habit of hurting citizens in bulk, whenever possible, and I had no reason to believe that this would be anything different.

"You think he might have wired the place up to blow?" Larsen asked.

"I think you know the prick as well as I do," was my reply.

Larsen hissed through his teeth, which were slightly discoloured from his C-Tab habit. "Fuck, Jack," he said. "Air support didn't pick anything up. This place would be glowing from up there if he'd set bombs."

"I don't want to risk it," I said, scanning the area around us. "People are going to die here today. You know that as well as I do. Our job is to keep the numbers low, and to get out of this alive."

"You talk about him as if he's a demon," Larsen said. "He's just a man."

I sighed. "Dante hasn't been just a man since his first kill." I removed my CPX-250 from its holster and checked its charge. Full to capacity. "You keep your eyes on him," I said, "but no one takes a shot. I don't want him down for good if he's got three-dozen citizens buried up to their necks in fucking quicksand."

"Comms?" Larsen said.

"He won't talk if he knows I'm wearing," I replied. "For some reason, he wants this to be between him and me."

"You've been chasing him through the past ten centuries," Larsen said. "Of *course* he wants it between you and him. He respects you, probably gets him hard knowing you're one step behind him all the way, but that doesn't mean you have to do this on your own, Jack. We're a squad, and we'll take him down if it means putting an end to his fucking kill-count."

I smiled. "I'm not alone, Larsen," I said, even though I was one step closer to being after that morning's argument with Laura.

"I'll have Dante for company." I patted my superior on the back and began to walk away, off toward the chess tables at the edge of the promenade, where Dante sat, patiently awaiting my arrival.

"Do you even know how to play chess?" Larsen called after me.

I shook my head. "How hard can it be?" I said, levelling my weapon toward Dante, who was waving at me nonchalantly, as if I was about to join him for drinks and conversation about pussy or sports.

Chess was the last thing on my mind.

Dante grinned at me as I drew near; it was a fake grin, for everything about Dante's face was fake. He wore a digital mask, which he must have picked up at some point in the future, and for as long as our little game of cat-and-mouse had been going on, he never took it off. Who knew what he looked like underneath that pixelated visage. For all I knew, Dante was a woman. For all I knew, Dante was King William, just having a bit of fun to kill the tedium of the monarchy.

"Don't you move a fucking muscle," I said, my gun trained upon his face, a face that some poor Chinese developer had probably spent countless years perfecting. "I swear to Christ, Dante, I'll shoot you where you sit."

He simply grinned wider. A shark's grin, which he must have asked the Chinese developer to put in so that one day he might unsettle the tortured agent, hell-bent on apprehending him. "There's no need for foul language," Dante said, hands held out in a placatory fashion. "Please, take a seat. We have a lot to discuss."

I could feel Larsen's eyes on me, and the eyes of the whole team. They were a long way away, but I knew at least ten of them had a clear shot. We'd had clear shots before, though. Dante was ostensibly bulletproof.

"Oh, come on," Dante said, his digitized mask shimmering in the early morning sunshine. "After all these years, all these centuries together, you don't have time to play one final game?" He motioned toward the chessboard; I could see he had set everything out to perfection. Every piece equidistant, not a speck of dust or gravel upon the board. It shouldn't have surprised me, for Dante had always been something of a perfectionist. I just never had him pegged as a fan of dreary board games.

"It's over," I told him.

"It's *dan* over, Jack," he said, and I shuddered. To hear my name falling from his lips was like nails down a chalkboard. All at once I felt light-headed, compromised, at risk of losing it. "Come on. Take a seat, play one game with me, and then, when we're done, regardless of who wins or loses, I'll let you take me in. No strings attached." He held up his arms, as if to prove he was no marionette. His armpits were sweaty, his green tee-shirt turned dark in places.

"And I'd really appreciate it if you'd put your gun away. Isn't it enough that Larsen's got you covered?" He smiled and pointed a long, slender finger off into the distance, to where my backup stood ready. They seemed to far way now, though. Might as well have not bothered turning up to the game.

"They'll shoot you," I said as I holstered my weapon. "You make any sudden moves, even look at me the wrong way, they'll fill you with so many rounds, the coroner will suggest a smelting instead of a cremation."

"I don't doubt it, Jack," he said, placing his hands down on the table, one either side of the chessboard. "Now, do you think we can get through this game without any further threats? What's one final hour amongst enemies? Hm? One last goodbye before I hand myself over for Cryo?"

I slowly took my seat, never once taking my eyes from Dante. It occurred to me that, in all the time I had been pursuing him, this was the closest I had ever been to the man. In 1499, we were in the same room — King Ferdinand II's boudoir — for the briefest of moments, but then Dante had dissolved before my eyes after setting a pre-travel sequence. In other words, he'd planned the whole thing down to the minutest of details. If Larsen hadn't come to my rescue, I would surely have been garrotted by the king's men, but that was the thing about Larsen: he always, always had my back.

"How many more people are going to die?" I asked, but Dante was too busy stroking his fake digital beard, which was there one second and gone the next. I wanted to reach across the table and strangle the life out of him, but I had a feeling that that was also what he wanted. An easy way out. The perfect way to draw a line beneath his crimes. His legacy would go on, and I would never know if he was telling the truth, that I could have put him in Cryo for the next thousand years, perhaps forever, where he would have suffered immensely for eternity. No, I wouldn't give him the easy way out he so desired. I would play him at his game, and send him to the chamber, where his own personal Hell awaited him.

"I hope you don't mind," he said, "but I figured you'd want to be whites. Whites are often working on behalf of the good, and blacks are, well, you're a lawman, you know how you feel about blacks." He laughed, and I despised him even more for it. "Winner takes all," he said, once he managed to compose himself. "By that, I mean if you win, I shall remove this digital mask and reveal to you something that has no doubt been eating you up inside all these years, but if I win, I keep it on forever, go the Cryo with you never knowing who it is you've been chasing."

"Either way, you're going down," I said. "Sounds good to me." I nudged my King a few millimetres to the left, just to bring some chaos to the board, and saw the disgust in Dante's face. It was my turn to smile.

"Whites always go first," he told me, which was a rule I never knew existed, but then again, as I had told Larsen, chess was never my game. I was more of a Monopoly guy, liked nothing more than to play a few games of Cluedo with George, whenever Laura allowed us some father-son time. "Let us begin."

Since I did not want to be sitting on the promenade all day, playing games with this twisted maniac, I wasted no time in making my first move: Queen's Pawn to D4. I had no idea whether that was a good move or not; I just wanted this to be over as soon as possible, and if that meant never knowing the true identity of Dante, well, I reckoned I could live with that.

"Ooweee!" he cried, rubbing his hands together maniacally. "This is going to be fun."

He made his move, his hand trembling with excitement as he shifted his King Pawn two spaces forward.

Larsen would be watching from afar, wondering what the fuck I was playing at, but he knew how much this meant to me. Dante had consumed me and my life for so long, what was one final game going to hurt if it meant putting him on ice for good.

And so we played. The game went on. He took one of mine, I took two of his. He took two of mine. I took one of his. Neither of us speaking; neither of us backing down. My heart racing within me, for I was so close… so very close…

I think Dante *wanted* me to win; he made several mistakes in quick succession, mistakes that I knew he was too smart to make, and I thought, *He wants me to know who he is. He wants to take off that damn digital mask, to reveal himself to me.* And I was right, because that was all part of his final game.

"I don't believe it," he said, suddenly, leaning away from the board after examining it thoroughly.

"What?" Whatever he saw, I did not.

The shark's grin returned. "You're a smart man, Jack," he said. "Take another look."

And so I looked, and it took me a few moments to realise that my Queen and Bishop had his King backed into a corner; no matter how he moved, we had him. It was checkmate. The game was over, and so was Dante.

But Dante didn't seem at all perturbed by his loss, or that he was about to spend eternity in Cryo—an infinitesimal price to pay for all the lives he had taken—and I knew then that he had thrown the game, for there was no fun in winning all of the time. The fun for him was only just starting, and it came with the removal of that hideous mask.

"Slowly," I said as he reached up to his face. I didn't think Larsen would take him out, not after the discussion we'd had prior to me coming out here, but there was always a chance one of his men would discern Dante's sudden movements as a threat, their sweat-slick finger already squeezing on the trigger.

"Okeedokeedoo," Dante said, and I thought nothing of it, because a lot of people still used that word, or some variation of it, but when Dante pushed a button beneath the right ear of his mask, and the digital masquerade flickered away, I looked into the eyes of the man before me, and in that moment I wanted Larsen to fire, to kill us both where we sat.

"No," I said. "No-no-no-no-no—"

The man who was once my little boy, my beautiful innocent George, smiled evilly. "I guess the divorce was the turning point," he said. "Oh, boy, it was all downhill after that."

He was talking about things that were yet to happen, the future, because that's where he was from, a future in which my son had murdered hundreds of people in the most despicable of ways. He had become Dante, and it was all my fault.

As I screamed out for Larsen, begged him to come and take this monster away from me, Dante—*George*—laughed until he was red in the face, and when he was finally done, and Larsen and his men were barrelling across the promenade toward us, he said simply one word to me.

"Checkmate."

It was almost dark when I arrived home. I sat in the car for a while, my fingers tightly gripping the steering wheel as Larsen's hologram sitting in the passenger seat watched me and smoked a C-Tab. Even though it was impossible, I thought I could smell the holographic smoke as it whorled around us both. It was sickly sweet, saccharine, and I hated it.

"None of this is your fault, Jack," Larsen assured me. "That little sonofabitch in there, he loves you—"

"That doesn't change things, Larsen," I said, gripping the wheel even tighter. "All those people, all those women and children, dead… because of George." I still couldn't believe it, didn't want to believe it. My entire life had come crashing down around me. "If I don't do something, it's going to happen all over again, whether Dante's in Cryo or not."

Larsen sighed. "You want to bring him in?" he said. "Bring George in, and we'll take care of it… somehow?"

I reached for the handle. "One life," I said, "to save three-hundred." A tear rolled down my cheek and alighted the corner of my mouth, its saltiness reminding me of trips to the beach in the summertime. George always loved the beach in the summertime.

"What are you going to do, Jack?"

I climbed out of the car and went into the house. Laura was upstairs, no doubt putting laundry in its rightful place. I could hear her pacing from room to room, cursing almost inaudibly to herself.

George was sat at the kitchen table, as if he hadn't budged since that morning, had been waiting for me to return in the exact same spot he'd been when I'd left.

"Daddy!" he cried, his face lighting up as he saw me, standing there in the doorway, one hand resting on my sidearm and tears rolling freely down my face now. "Daddy, whatsamatter? Why do you look so sad?"

I told him I loved him.

And then I saved three-hundred lives.

Adam's Afterword

"The first thing I saw when I looked at the image I was given was time-travel. It might have had something to do with those warped sides, the almost convex nature of the right and left. Then, of course, the checkerboard design could only mean one thing: chess. Chess and time-travel? How hard could it be, right? Turned out to be a lot more difficult than I thought, but I hope I managed to pull it off. I'll let you decide."

TEN MINUTE WARNING

EM DEHANEY

When it finally happened, after all the false alarms, all the scare tactics and practice drills and meals eaten from tins, breathing in each other's air for a few hours and thinking it a great adventure, when the siren finally sounded for real, we froze, paralysed as our pockets vibrated in simultaneous warning.

Would there be retaliation? Had the submarine commanders already confirmed the launch codes as we scurried into our well-stocked basement?

Would the warhead be shot out of the sky before it even reached us? Our allies were dwindling, and the ongoing war had left our defence budgets in tatters. Who would come to our rescue? Were we worth rescuing?

Would we feel the blast? We knew the missile was on its way, but where would it hit? A city? A village? A hospital? A school?

What would be the biggest killer? The fireball blast? The vaporising flash of light? The tonnes of dirt raining down from the mushroom cloud?

We were told to hide.

Hide and wait.

The fallout would be at its worst in the first two weeks, so the leaflets said. Plutonium particles carry for hundreds of miles on the nuclear winds, and I imagined them as sparkling dandelion seeds, dancing in the poisonous air outside. Our lungs would fill with the dust from a thousand cremated bones of our fellow country-men and women.

We had bottled water. We had board games and playing cards. We had blankets and pillows. We had first-aid kits with eye-baths and finger bandages and safety pins. We had each other.

So we waited.

The chemical toilet couldn't cope with all the corned beef and peaches we were eating, and blocked up around Day Five. The passing of the days was hard to gauge. My dad had covered up the tiny basement fanlight window with breeze blocks. We had battery-powered storm lamps for when the electricity went out. We yearned for daylight, for sun and clouds and oxygen.

Still we waited, our own stench filling our nostrils. We sponged our bodies down with disposable wet-wipes, which we piled into a plastic bag and left in the corner. The cot beds were uncomfortable, and every time I tried to sleep, I was woken by the old chimpanzee reflex that stops you falling from the trees. My eyes opening with a jolt. I would see my father sat, staring at the pile of dried food packets. He seemed never to sleep, or he slept with his eyes open. I never could tell.

My brother was sick one day after a meal. We stopped calling them lunch, breakfast, dinner. Those labels were meaningless. Rice pudding, thick, white and lumpy, like scrambled brains, came shooting out of his mouth and nose. My mother leapt to help him, cleaned him up, and laid him down on his little bed. She thought I didn't see the looks passed over his head to my father, but I saw. I saw everything. We all did, down in that basement, together, all the time.

They said two weeks was safe, and to listen to the radio for news.

We took a wind-up radio down there, but in all our drills and tests and play-acting the nuclear holocaust, we never stopped to check it actually worked. Faulty wiring, my dad said. In a way, I was glad. What would the radio say? Would it tell us how many died? How many lived? Or, even worse, would we crank the handle, build up enough charge, just for the radio to spew static back at us, mocking us with Geiger-counter cackles.

My mother brushed her hair and put on lipstick for the first few days, then the lips stayed bare, then the hair started to knot. When she tried to comb it, a limp, golden lock fell away in her hand. She hid it under her pillow, of all places. Perhaps she hoped the tooth fairy would take pity on her.

She didn't touch her hair after that.

My brother and I soon exhausted the supply of games, so we started to make up our own. Above ground, our age gap meant we were distant, strangers living in the same house. I found him annoying, he found me boring. At fifteen I was too old to want his spotty thirteen-year-old face around. But down here, in the possible prelude to the end of the world, or at least the world as we knew it, we became best friends again, like when we were small. We climbed around the room, pretending the floor was radioactive ooze, much to our parents' horror. We gave each other impossible "Would you rather…" challenges that made our mother blush and our father chuckle into his beard. I taught him silly dance routines and he shared his never-ending supply of knock-knock jokes.

When my father had counted fourteen periods of awake and asleep, he thought it safest to stay put, just for a while. We had no concept of day or night, hot or cold, apocalypse or lucky escape.

So we waited.

We had enough food for months. All I wanted was an orange. I would lie in my cot, dreaming of peeling the fruit, piercing it with my thumb nail, the mist of citrus oil coating my skin. Of taking a bite, shredding the delicate flesh between my teeth. Of juice running down my chin and dripping onto the floor, despite my slurps and swallows.

I began to wonder what could grow from the nuclear ashes. Like volcanos producing fertile soil to nourish plants and trees, would this new scorched and dead earth eventually bring forth fruit? Would the pears droop on their branches, heavy with toxic sludge? Would the vineyards grow curly tendrils thick with bunches of blackened grapes that would burst like fish-eyes in your mouth? Would the carrots and potatoes buried underground claw their way out like zombies from their graves, white fingers of blight and mould facilitating their mobility?

I watched my brother. He watched me. He was hiding something under his blanket, I knew it. I saw my dad eyeing my brother's cot. He knew it too. What was under there? We subtly surveilled each other, never catching the other's eye, but aware all the same. He began talking to my mother in code. Although the surface conversations were about the water situation or if we would eat the tinned potato salad or the luncheon meat, it was obvious they were talking about me. They were planning something.

My brother was in on it too.

I had a revelation. He was hiding weapons; weapons we would surely need when we emerged into the wasteland of radiation survival. Guns and ammo? Maybe something more practical. A machete? An axe? Why had my parents entrusted my brother with our safety? He was too young. I was taller and braver. I should be the one to bear arms when we escaped our basement prison.

When the storm lamps were turned down low and my family's breathing had become shallow and deep, I crawled out of my cot, slithered across the floor and ran a hand under my brother's blanket. He grabbed my wrist. His eyes shone in the semi-darkness.

'I know you are in on it with them,' he hissed in my ear. 'I'm watching you.'

I melted back to my own lair, planning my next move. His eyes remained open, staring at me. Now I knew why they had given him the axe. It must be an axe, no-one would give a gun to a child; that would be ridiculous. They had given him the axe to protect himself from me. I could hear them now, tapping Morse code messages to each other on the walls and the floor. One tap for Kill Her Now.

Two taps for Wait.

Luckily I could understand them. I wouldn't be the one who waited to be slaughtered in my own bed.

My mother coughed.

That was the signal.

The tapping grew more intense.

A shaft of blue light opened up as I leapt from my bed to charge at my brother, raining down blows on his head with a can of condensed milk. His screams were drowned by the thundering of steps and the roar of shouting. Gloved hands pulled me away. Hazmat suits and helmets filled the room.

We were saved.

My brother was bleeding from his nose and mouth.

He never woke up.

But at least the war was over.

Em's Afterword

"To me, the image looked like an apocalyptic explosion, a nuclear mushroom cloud seen from above. North Korea were deep in their warhead testing cycle and the news story about the false nuclear warning in Hawaii had recently been on the TV, so I started researching warning systems and government safety advice for the event of an atomic bomb. Then I started to think about what might happen if you were trapped in a makeshift bunker with your family for weeks on end, not knowing what was happening in the outside world. Of course, it would end in paranoia and murder. Well, it would with my family anyway."

UNCOMMON TIME

JOHN McNEE

Landing a helicopter in a blizzard was no easy task, but Masha seemed not to notice or care, except during moments when the turbulence interfered with the reading of her magazine.

"Do try a bit harder not to get us killed, won't you Helmut?" she chided the pilot. "That is what I pay you for."

"Sorry Mrs Stroyberg," he answered, wrestling with the controls. "We're coming in now."

"Well it's about time," she said, slipping her reading glasses into the inside pocket of her fur coat, folding the magazine away and checking her make-up in the passenger-side vanity mirror she had requested be installed. She pursed her lips ruefully at the vision. The rouge and mascara were fine, but it was the skin beneath that displeased her. Too many lines around the eyes, too much sagging at the jaw. "Getting old," she muttered, so quietly only she could hear it and spot it for the lie it was. She was already old. What she was getting was *ancient*.

The helicopter bounced twice on the snow-covered lawn before coming to a rest. "We're down," Helmut announced, his hands shaking, sweat smeared across his brow. It sounded like he could hardly believe it.

"Oh really? I hadn't noticed." Masha was staring ahead towards the building on the hill. Its square, black edifice loomed intermittently through the frozen flurries.

"Is that the house?" Helmut asked, squinting. "For a rock star I'd have expected something more... ostentatious?"

"Ugly," Masha muttered and slipped out of her safety belt.

"If you wait a few moments I can escort you..."

"Certainly not. You can stay here. I might want to leave in a hurry." She ignored his despairing expression as she climbed down onto the snow, still circulating in tornadoes all around her, whipped up by the spinning rotor blades.

When she was a few feet in front of the helicopter she spotted the blue lamps lining the path to the house and followed them to a front door that was as flat and blank as the rest of the building. She managed to find the bell, rang it, and after a moment, the door swung slowly inward, its automated mechanisms emitting a low electronic hum.

"Gauche," she muttered.

She entered a long, black hallway with what appeared to be only one exit, other than the door behind her. No-one came to greet her, but she could hear light piano music from the room up ahead – a subtle invitation to enter. Following it, she emerged into a large, square, split-level living room with no windows, entirely decorated in black and white. From where she stood, steps led down to a seating area and a marble fireplace. A pair of sofas – one black, one white – stood either end of a chequered tile floor. At its centre was a white stone plinth on which stood a single black cube, the size of a jewellery box.

The split layout made her feel like she was walking out onto a nightclub stage, compounded by the fact that a number of instruments had been arranged to her left. A piano, drums and double bass were positioned around a chrome microphone. All were still waiting to be put to use, except for the piano, which was being played by a young woman in a black party dress, her naked back turned to Masha.

The tune was choppy. A series of overcomplicated riffs in search of a melody. *One for the technical crowd*, Masha thought. *Too clever for its own good.*

"Hello?"

"Hello," the girl answered, without slowing her fingers or turning round.

"I'm Masha Stroyberg."

The girl said nothing.

"I was invited here by Lillian Lund."

The girl said nothing.

"Rude," Masha muttered, before clearing her throat and raising her voice. "Is Lillian here?"

"She'll be down shortly." The girl nodded to the cocktail trolley against the opposite wall. "Make yourself a drink."

"Insolent," Masha muttered, casting an eye back down the hall, thinking how easy it would be to leave. *But you're here now*, she thought, turning back to regard the plinth and the curious black cube. *Might as well find out what this is all about.*

She crossed the room to reach the drinks trolley, getting a better view of the piano player as she did. She was late teens or early 20s, of apparently Asian descent and beautiful, with skin so fair and hair so dark that she complemented the décor of the room. She never looked up, instead keeping her eyes on the keys as her fingers drummed across them, hammering out dazzlingly intricate phrases that repeated and repeated and repeated up and down in cascading waves of modulation apparently positioned to be as disruptive and counter-intuitive as possible. An exercise in complexity designed to entertain the performer rather than the audience.

"You're giving me a headache," Masha announced. "Can't you play something that swings?"

The girl halted her performance immediately, considered the request for a moment, then began playing something new. A pseudo jazz ballad that switched back and forth between melodies and time signatures every few bars, like a competition between compositions. Not what Masha had in mind, but better than what preceded it.

She poured herself a vodka tonic and paced the length of the room, examining the paintings on the walls. She preferred not to venture down into the pit – as she had immediately come to think of it – with its odd black cube. She didn't know what it was, beyond the symbolism, but that was reason enough to be wary of it. Black cubes and hexagons had also found their way into all of the paintings on the wall, most of which appeared to be representations of Saturn in one interpretation or another. Masha sipped her drink as she pondered the implications. Her own interest in the occult and ritual magic – what little had ever been genuine – had dissipated long ago. Lillian, it appeared, was still an ardent believer and practitioner.

"And who are you?" Masha asked of the girl. "Am I allowed to know?"

"My name is Kuriko Takahashi. I play piano."

"Yes, I can see that. But it doesn't tell me much."

"I began playing at age two and performing concerts at three. At seven years old I made my debut at the Tokyo Opera City Concert Hall with the Japanese Philharmonic Orchestra performing Rachmaninoff's Third Piano Concerto. I toured in the United States, Russia and France, before accepting an offer to study at the Royal Danish Music Conservatory, at nine years old."

Masha shrugged. "Never heard of you."

"I grew up. When I was nine I was a child prodigy. Now I'm 23, I'm just a piano player."

I could happily murder this girl, Masha thought. *To be so young, so talented, so beautiful, and be complaining about the cruelties of old age.* "None of the philharmonics want you now?"

"I gave up classical music a long time ago." Kuriko never stopped playing, but waited for breaks or slow sections in the tune before speaking. It made for a halting, frustrating conversation. "Too easy. Jazz is more exciting. Improvisation more challenging."

"Sure. But it can be tough finding friends to play with."

Now Kuriko looked up, facing Masha for the first time. She stopped playing, dropped her hands into her lap and looked away. "I don't mind playing alone."

I've upset her, Masha thought, feeling proud of herself. "You know, I was in a band, once."

Kuriko turned back to face her, frowning.

"You didn't know that?"

Kuriko shook her head.

"There were four of us. Myself on vocals, Lillian on bass, of course, and two others. An all-female avant-garde jazz-rock quartet. You think such things are rare today, you should have been there in 1967. *No-one* was ready for us. I suppose that was part of the problem." She swirled the ice around in her glass and took another drink. It was almost finished, already. "Tarnished Neon – that was what we called ourselves. It was a wonderful experience, while it lasted."

"What happened?"

"The same thing that often happens." Masha cast an eye around the room. "It stopped being about the music. Became something...*else*. I need another drink."

"I'll get it!" The voice came from behind her.

Masha turned to face a woman she hadn't seen in decades. Lillian Lund sashayed across the room in a ball gown as white as her hair. Its natural lack of colour was a clear indicator of her advancing years, but any other evidence of the ravages of time was barely noticeable. Her skin was smooth, her bare arms toned, waist thin and stride proud.

The sight made Masha physically sick. She hugged her coat a little tighter about herself, wanting to expose as little of her own failing body as possible. "Lillian. It's nice of you to join us."

"Sorry for keeping you waiting," Lillian said as she filled two glasses. "I wanted everything to be perfect and perfection takes time, as well you know."

"Indeed," Masha swapped her old drink for a fresh one when it was offered to her. "You look incredible."

Lillian waved her hand. "Let's not say such things. It will only end up reminding us of how many years we've been apart."

That's a sneaky way to avoid returning the compliment, Masha thought. "Fine. In that case, why don't you tell me what I'm doing here?"

"Kuriko!" Lillian snapped her fingers. "Play something! We need atmosphere."

The girl responded immediately, launching into a boogie-woogie that quickly deviated towards the baroque. Meade Lux Lewis by way of Bach. Masha thought it was, by far, the best thing the prodigy had played yet.

"Have you met?" Lillian asked.

"We've spoken."

"I was quite prepared to scour the entire globe to find the greatest pianist in the world. And it turned out she was living in Copenhagen! All I had to do was send a taxi! Isn't that insane?"

"Serendipitous. Are you putting a new band together? I thought you were enjoying retirement."

"I haven't retired," Lillian said, taking offence. "Creto split up, that's all." This was in reference to the rock group she'd co-founded in 1978, 10 years after the dissolution of Tarnished Neon.

35 years of critical acclaim and financial success followed, till others in the band decided it was time to bring it to a conclusion. The rock'n'roll lifestyle wasn't quite as much fun after 70, they'd decided. "Anyway, it's not a *new* group I'm thinking of putting together, but an old one."

"Tarnished Neon? You're not serious."

"I thought you'd be excited."

"That's why I'm here? *That's* why you sent me your cryptic bloody blackmail note? So I could help you relive your glory days?"

"*Your* glory days. I'm already living *my* glory days."

Masha's laugh was one of exasperation more than humour. "You're teasing me."

Lillian smiled, mischievously. "Perhaps. It's fun to see each other again, isn't it?"

"Why *am* I here?"

Lillian waved an arm around the room. "Well for one thing, I thought it was about time you saw the new pad. Cost a fortune to build, but I had to have everything just so."

"No windows."

"If I need to see outside I can *go* outside."

"And no-one can see in, which I suppose must be convenient." She eyed the pianist. "What about Kuriko? How does she feel about performing in a satanic temple?"

Kuriko stumbled over her notes, but didn't stop playing.

Lillian pursed her lips and tutted. "Now who's teasing?"

"Look at the floor, Kuriko. Look at the paintings. Look at *that*." Masha pointed at the black cube. "This whole room is an altar to the Devil. Primed for a blood sacrifice."

Now Kuriko did stop playing.

"Don't listen to her," said Lillian. "She's being characteristically over the top. Honestly, Masha. Satan and devilry. What a way to twist the truth. You should know better, as someone who was once an active participant."

"I don't recall much about it."

"Really? I remember it all perfectly."

"Maybe I have a bad memory."

"Or a guilty conscience."

"What does that mean?"

The chime of the doorbell interrupted their back-and-forth.

"Our final guest, at last." Lillian began marching out into the hall. "Not a word 'til I return!"

They listened to the fading click of Lillian's heels for a few moments, before Kuriko said, "Does she really worship Satan?"

Masha looked at the cube, pondering its blank surface. "She worships Saturn. Thinks it holds dominion over our universe. That it has the power to grant whatever one desires."

"Oh. Not the Devil?"

Masha turned towards the girl and showed her the closest thing she could muster to a sympathetic smile. "There's no such thing, dear. They're all just stories. Like Lillian said, I was... teasing."

"Oh." Kuriko thought for a moment. "Why did you tell me to look at the floor?"

Masha cast an eye over the tiles. "The chequerboard floor is common to numerous temples in various religions, dating back thousands of years. They say it represents duality, the balance of good and evil, and beyond that, our physical realm. It is also, some have claimed, a portal, connecting energies between universes. If you want to commune with a power beyond humanity, it helps to be standing on that floor. I wasn't lying about blood sacrifices, by the way."

Laughter from the hallway. The sound of two pairs of heels on approach. Kuriko began to play again just before Lillian threw open the door to announce the new arrival. "And here she is!"

The woman who walked in was half a foot shorter than Masha and twice as heavy, with dark skin, red heels and a red dress. A mink stole was around her shoulders and a broad grin was on her face. "Bless my soul," she said. "If it ain't *the* Masha Frandsen!"

Masha smiled, thinly. "Stroyberg now. And for some time."

"Oh, of course." The woman laughed, deep and soulful. "How could I forget?"

"Hello Angela."

"That's no way to say hello. Come here!" Angela closed the distance between them in three big strides, throwing her arms open wide and wrapping them around Masha, nearly crushing her in her fierce embrace. "I've missed you, you skinny bitch!"

"Likewise," Masha managed to gasp, though in truth she hadn't thought of Angela Dumont in decades. A talented percussionist from Georgia, she had been sent to study in Denmark in the mid-60s, where she had become the drummer for Tarnished Neon. She had remained in Europe for many years afterwards, playing with one group or another, before returning home and marrying an Alabama preacher with his own touring band and TV show.

"What a sight," Lillian remarked, stepping past the pair to make another visit to the drinks trolley. "It warms the heart to see old friends reunited."

"Then this *is* a reunion," said Masha, as Angela released her before descending into the pit and the comfort of the white sofa.

"Of a sort," Lillian admitted.

"Sounds good to me," Angela said. "All I've played for too long is gospel music."

Masha scoffed. "Hallelujah."

"Masha please," Lillian said, nodding towards the plinth. "Not in front of the cube."

Masha let out a cry of exasperation and threw up her hands. "What *is* the damn cube?" She stepped down onto the tiles and approached the plinth, directing a thin finger at the object perched atop it. "Feel like it's been staring at me from the moment I walked in."

"Don't touch it," said Lillian. "I'm warning you."

"I want some answers!"

"You'll get them. Everyone's here. We can begin right away, if you're ready."

"Begin what?"

Lillian abandoned the drinks, walked over to the instruments, crouched down behind the double bass and stood up holding a stack of crisp, freshly-printed sheet music.

Masha let out a sarcastic laugh. "You honestly expect us to perform one of our old songs?"

"This isn't old." Lillian waved the sheets in her hand. "This is new. A never-before performed song by Sofia Good."

The name was enough to stun both Masha and Angela into silence.

Kuriko was compelled to ask, "Who is Sofia Good?"

I was afraid of this, Masha thought. *Exactly this.*

"Tell her," Lillian said. Her expression was hard. Insistent.

Masha cleared her throat. "Sofia was... the pianist in Tarnished Neon."

"And composer of all the songs," said Angela. "It began and ended with Sofia."

"What do you mean?" asked Kuriko.

"She died," said Lillian.

"Suicide," said Masha.

"That's what they called it, anyway," said Angela.

This is it, Masha thought. *Fifty years late, they're finally going to put me on trial for something I didn't even do.*

"She asphyxiated, slowly, on a cocktail of hydrogen, helium, methane and ammonia," said Lillian. "No method of how it got into her lungs was ever uncovered."

"They called it suspicious circumstances," said Angela.

"She was depressed," said Masha.

"Heartbroken," said Angela. "One of her best friends had just stolen her lover."

"Bullshit," Masha spat, rounding on the other woman. "There was nothing between Max and me till after Sofia died." This was a lie. But it was a lie she had held to for five decades, so wasn't about to give it up. The truth was that she had wanted Sofia's fiancé Max Stroyberg, heir to the Stroyberg fortune, for herself and had plotted to steal him away. She had succeeded on the day Sofia took her own life.

"Plenty of suspicion at the time," Angela said, clearly enjoying herself. "Plenty of rumours."

"There was a suicide note," said Masha.

"A single line," said Lillian. "Who can wage war against the beast?" The same line had been on the invitation Masha had received. Just that, a date, an hour and Lillian's address.

"Revelations," said Angela. "Chapter 13, verse 4."

"The beast?" Kuriko's voice was a fearful squeak.

Lillian smiled down at her. "It's a metaphor, dear."

"Yes," said Masha, trying to hide her shaking hands. "For depression."

"Or betrayal," Angela suggested, laying it on thick, eyes on Masha, letting her know she couldn't just brush off her portion of blame.

"Neither," said Lillian. "It's time. Time was the beast. Always was. Still is."

"What the hell are you talking about?" Masha was growing incensed.

"I'll tell you," said Lillian, cool and measured as ever. "If you let me. If you just shut your mouth, I'll tell you everything."

Biting her tongue, Masha took a seat on the edge of the sofa, next to Angela, and waved for Lillian to continue. Lillian nodded in gratitude and took a breath.

"For a time, we all worshipped Saturn." This she delivered to Kuriko, gifting her knowledge the girl was clearly uncomfortable to be receiving. "It began with Sofia. Where the rest of us were led to the true Lord of Time and Space through music, for her it was the opposite. She understood music to be the language of the universe and that was what led her to us. She formed our little group to perform her hymns in uncommon time."

"She tricked you?" asked Kuriko.

Lillian shook her head. "We knew what we were doing. Sofia was a savant, touched by a world beyond ours. She understood the darkness at the heart of Saturn, and how to converse with it. When she spoke of the rewards – the tangible, physical gains – it was impossible to be unmoved or unconvinced. We all had our own requests. Our hearts hungry with desire for rewards material and spiritual – wealth, fame, fulfilment. We performed the songs Sofia composed. Ritual in every note. Invocation in every beat of the bar. And we got it all. Everything we asked for."

Masha rolled her eyes. "Oh, give me strength! There's not the slightest shred of proof that anything we ever said or did..."

Kuriko was the one who cut in with the pertinent question. "What did Sofia want?"

Masha didn't protest the interruption. She wanted to hear the answer herself.

Lillian shook her head. "She never told us. But then, about five years ago, I received a package."

What is this now? Masha thought. *What manner of fresh torture is this?*

"Inside was a note from Sofia's lawyers, sheet music for half a song... and *that*." Lillian pointed at the cube and smiled. "Did you really mean what you said earlier? About feeling like it was watching you?"

Masha stood. "You think it's *her*?"

"The lawyer's note was light on details," Lillian said. "Apparently the cube and the music were found with Sofia's body. She left instructions that both were to be concealed for 45 years, then sent to me. Police did analyse it at the time of her death and concluded that it was a block of solid carbon, about as mystical as a paperweight."

"And what the hell do you think it is?"

"Time was Sofia's greatest fear. Her most dreadful enemy. She didn't want to grow old, like us. She didn't want to wither and die. And she didn't see it as an inevitability. She was determined to overcome it. I don't believe she ever died. I believe she left this realm on a journey to free herself of mortality. And I believe *that* to be the vessel through which she will return."

There was silence for several seconds. And then Masha laughed, genuinely, for the first time that evening. "I understand now! You're just mad! Oh, that's a relief!"

Lillian, unfazed, raised the music above her head. "The name of this song is 'Resurrection'. It was half-finished at the time of Sofia's apparent death in 1968. After I received the cube, it was found to be emitting a vibration. A subsonic hum – below the range of human hearing – that changed in frequency at irregular intervals over the course of the next five years, ceasing just two months ago. When the sequence was recorded and transposed to the key of the original song, it matched perfectly and continued where the original left off."

"What are you saying?" asked Angela.

"The prayer of resurrection," said Lillian. "Written half in this world, half in the next. If we perform it – all of us, together, here and now... I believe she will return."

Masha was still laughing. "You're insane. Completely insane." She coughed, wiped the tears from her eyes, then stood and held out her hand. "But fine. If it'll help wrap things up, just give me my part."

Lillian handed over the relevant pages and looked to Angela. "Will you?"

The other woman sighed and rose slowly from the sofa, tugging at the stole around her shoulders. "I can't say I'm comfortable doing it. It's not who I am now. But you're right that I owe a debt to Sofia. We all do."

"Thank you," Lillian said.

They each took their music and their places on the stage. They would be performing directly to the cube, the music confined within the walls of Lillian's personal temple.

"What is happening?" Kuriko asked timidly, glancing over the notes as they were placed before her, her own fingers moving instinctively to replicate them. "I don't understand."

"It's perfectly simple." Masha smiled, putting on her reading glasses and taking her place behind the mic. "We're going to play a song to raise the dead."

"Oh." Kuriko now appeared supremely uncomfortable.

"Just play the notes as written, dear," Lillian advised. "Angela, would you start us off?"

She did, teasing the rhythm out on the cymbals before attacking the snares. Seven beats in the measure – accent on the first and fifth beats in the bar. A little off-kilter, but not difficult to pick up. Lillian found her own groove quickly enough. Kuriko played her part with perfect precision – a parade of simple, sombre phrases in minor key.

The lyrics were written phonetically. A language that Masha didn't understand, had never investigated, but had been told, long ago, was Sanskrit. She felt a pang of nostalgia on seeing the opening phrase, as she opened her mouth to sing. After 50 years, her singing voice was the only part of her that hadn't aged. The notes she held were pure – golden.

She felt the joy of the song as it came together, its spirit awakening parts of her she hadn't felt in years. She sang out, exalting in the energy as it flowed through her, feeling the notes before she saw them, knowing the words before she read them.

They were, for a period of around five minutes, united in the warmth and darkness of the music.

Then she glanced up from the pages, saw the cube was gone, and screamed.

The performance ended immediately, the others shocked into silence.

"What is it?" Angela asked.

Masha pointed ahead to the plinth – empty now, but slick with black oil. It coated the floor beneath, expanding out across the tiles in a perfect circle.

"It's her," Lillian whispered, awestruck. "It worked."

The cube was liquid now. Moving.

"Like Hell," Masha spat, her eyes on the dark pool spreading out beneath her. *I can't be here for this.*

Lillian stepped out from behind the double bass. "Masha…"

"I'm leaving."

"You can't." Lillian reached out a hand towards her. "Not yet. We need..."

And Masha, turning to face her, put a hand in her fur coat and drew the revolver. "Get back!" She thrust the gun forward, aiming it at Lillian's chest. "Don't touch me!"

"Masha..."

"Do you think I don't know what comes next?" Her frantic eyes darted between Lillian and Angela. "I won't be your sacrifice!"

Angela was on her feet now. All four were on their feet. "Masha, what the hell did you bring a gun for?"

"Because I knew you would be plotting against me!" Masha's hands quivered as she yelled. "You *always* blamed me!"

Lillian, hands raised, voice straining for calm, nodded her head. "I did. For a long time. But that was before I learned the truth. Haven't you been listening?"

"She's out of her damn mind," said Angela. "This is what 50 years of guilt does to a person."

"It changes nothing!" There was froth on Masha's lips. "I remember how the old songs ended. The ritual. In blood. There was *always* blood!"

Closing her eyes for a moment, Lillian inhaled deeply and let it out in a long sigh. "On that point, you are correct, dear Masha. There has to be blood."

Lillian's hands moved too fast for Masha's to catch, closing around the gun and wrenching it up. Masha was caught out, but didn't let go. She lunged, throwing her body into Lillian's as she tried to pull the weapon away from her.

"Angela!" Lillian cried. And there was an almighty crash of drums and cymbals as the other woman kicked her way through and grabbed for Masha, putting her in a bear hug twice as strong as the one from before, squeezing the air out of her lungs and the blood from her limbs.

Masha wanted to scream and fight but didn't have strength to do either. She felt the revolver ripped from her grasp as Lillian disentangled herself from the melee.

They'll kill me now, Masha thought, shrieking inside her head. *These hags. These bitches. These contemptible, miserable, spiteful...*

There was a clatter as Lillian tossed the pistol into a corner, then strode towards Kuriko.

The pianist was shaking from panic at the edge of the stage, hugging herself. "What's happening?" she asked. "I don't understand. I'm scared."

"Don't be scared," Lillian told her, put her hands on her shoulders and gave her a forceful shove into the pit.

The girl didn't scream. All she emitted was a gasp of confused despair as she fell, almost politely, into the darkness. Her body dropped instantly beneath the surface, plummeting like a stone in a well of black ink. No ripples were cast. She was, quite simply, in the world one moment, out of it the next.

Angela, horrified, released her hold on Masha to make the sign of the cross.

Sucking air into her lungs, Masha dropped to her knees. "Why?"

Lillian's gaze remained fixed on the void below them – its seeping promise of endless, elegant darkness. "We're asking a lot here," she said, her voice flat. "Breaking the laws of the universe. Waging war against the beast. Big demands come at a heavy cost. How much would you say *your* decrepit old soul is worth?"

Masha shivered and sniffed, feeling tears spring to her eyes. "Mean," she muttered.

Lillian returned her gaze to the floor, but the darkness was gone.

Masha dropped her head into her hands, unable to choke back the sobs, imagining the sight of herself – a pitiful old woman, weeping on her knees. And then she heard the voice. They all heard it.

"Besides, if we lost you, we'd have to recruit a new vocalist. And that would be a massive pain in the ass." She spoke from behind the piano, punctuating her words with a delicate flurry across the keys.

From her position on the floor, Masha couldn't see who the voice belonged to. She could only see the reactions of the others. Angela – mouth agape, disbelieving. Lillian – smiling through her tears.

Wiping her eyes, Masha clambered up onto her feet, staggered towards the piano and confirmed the impossible sight. Sofia Good – young, beautiful, resurrected, immortal – sat at the keyboard, satin dress clinging to her angelic frame, auburn hair pinned with silver. Her fingers danced out the introduction to a tune they all knew by heart.

"Come on, ladies," she said, through a grin as wide as the night sky. "That Old Black Magic. I'll play you in."

She didn't have to say anymore. They shuffled quickly, wordlessly back to their positions. Lillian to the double bass. Angela hastily rebuilding her drum kit. Masha clearing her throat on approach to the microphone.

Not a glance was shared. Not a moment of horror about what was taking place and all that led to it. Whatever they had done, whatever was to come, none of it was important in this moment.

All that mattered was the music and the chance to play together, as they once had, long ago.

When they were *young*.

John's Afterword

"I may have too literal a mind for this kind of project. I admit I studied the piece of art I was sent for some time, expecting something definitive to materialise from the patterns. But it didn't. What I saw was a black square surrounded by black and white shapes in a kind of vortex or portal. So that's what I worked with. A black cube at the centre of the picture led me to put a black cube at the centre of the story. It kind of looked like a black house in the middle of a blizzard, so that was the setting. The black and white patterns around the cube looked like helicopter rotors, so that influenced the opening. They also looked like piano keys, so a piano player had to be a key character. The patterns appeared to be divided into four sections, so that meant four main characters – a musical quartet. The black cube is the symbol of Saturn Worship, a kind of ritual black magic, so that seemed an obvious element to incorporate, along with the religious and magical symbolism of the chequerboard floor. And staring very closely at the centre of the picture, I thought I could see something in the cube. Something that vaguely resembled the shape of a woman. And the rest just... fell into place."

EXILE IN EXTREMIS

PAULA D. ASHE

From: DDennis@reviledmag.com "David Dennis"

To: ELLE@abyssus.net "ELLE Unknown"

Subject: Re: Priest of Breathing Piece

Date: 9.25.XX at 9:13am

I'm gonna skip any and all pleasantries since the police are getting involved. Jesus. Who knew a weird little story about grave-robber barons of suburbia would turn into a fucking manhunt for Cay Castleton III? I won't insult you by asking again if the story's true; our fact-checkers verified everything a week before the story went live. I think I'm just writing that out again to make myself feel better. I guess when I imagined some creep paying another creep to 'resurrect' his dead wife, I just figured it was some anonymous nobody. Not the heir apparent to the Castleton Empire. Like, what the actual fuck is happening in this town? How'd you even come up with the idea for this story?

Anyway, it's nothing too serious at this point, just thinly veiled threats about subpoenas and warrants and other shit. Since I have no "identifying information" about you other than your email address and Venmo account, you shouldn't be bothered. I just wanted to give you a head's up since they're asking a lot of questions about you and your sources. I shouldn't mention this but I'm sort of freaking out.

Dave

David Dennis

Managing Editor

Reviled Magazine

From: ELLE@abyssus.net "ELLE Unknown"

To: DDennis@reviledmag.com "David Dennis"

Subject: Re: Re: Priest of Breathing Piece

Date: 9.25.XX at 11:22am

David,

Thank you for your message. Feel free to share the audio files and/or transcripts of my interviews should the police request them.

As to your question, I ply my trade in revealing the depraved. Nothing surprises me anymore, especially when it involves sex and conservative politicians. I did a piece for another underground publication a few years ago about a (male) state senator (a real Family Values type) who was found dead beneath a (male) putrefying corpse. The kicker? The corpse was tumescent inside the senator. EMTs had to... separate them. The rumors spanned everything from *True Detective*-like occult conspiracies to an underground market in cadavers for closet cases ('no homo' if the other dude is dead, right?). To this day – I monitor the outcomes of every story I write – nobody has yet provided a solid explanation about how a carcass managed to get inside the senator's estate, bedroom, bed, and body. Real-life rapist zombies sounds like just the sort of story Reviled readers would love, does it not? Sadly, my connection to that story is no longer speaking to me.

As for answers, I have none. None that would make reasonable sense, anyway. I wanted to find out more about the spate of break-ins at St. Julian's Cemetery. I initially presumed some impoverished junkies were bribing their security staff. When I realized that all the break-ins were of mausoleums, and that the bodies themselves (three at that point) were gone, I had to use some unorthodox methods to track down the sorts of people who would be in the 'female corpse recirculation' racket. It should not surprise you that there are many. What caught my attention was that the people responsible for the abductions were formerly betrothed to the remains. They did nothing to hide their tracks, aside from paying in cash, which is also traceable if one has... the necessary skillset to do so. Thankfully (I suppose?) my methods are the kind that law enforcement have no mind or use for, so I am not concerned there. In fact, Cay Castleton Cubed has only been mentioned in the comment threads of the article and the police have been rousting those folks ever since. It is not their fault that

Castleton's tragically deceased ladylove was found decomposing in a squalid flat in Kedger's Point, propped up in their nuptial bed with glistening cat entrails dangling from her Botox-injected lips.

You and your publication are fine. Do not let the police scare you with their bluster. I can assure you, there are far worse things in the world, in our own backyards even, than bureaucrats with badges.

There is someone in our city called the 'Priest of Breathing' who is somehow convincing otherwise rational people that he alone can revive their loved ones from the dead. If it is any consolation, I have not slept much since penning this story.

ELLE

From: SLim@reviledmag.com "Scott Lim"

To: ELLE@abyssus.net "ELLE Unknown"

CC: DDennis@reviledmag.com "David Dennis"

Subject: Police Investigation Protocol

Date: 9.25.XX at 1:13pm

Hello Elle,

I'm Scott Lim, President and CEO of Reviled Media. Your story, "'Til Death': Inside the Real-Life Resurrection Cult in Anchorite City" has become quite the viral sensation! I wanted to touch basis with you to establish a protocol for the police investigation that has resulted in light of the publication of your article. As you know, all contacted journalists sign a waiver indicating that should a police investigation arise as result of their work, they will cooperate fully with any and all law enforcement in perpetuty. After 31 days online, we're at 212M views and counting. Reviled Mag's V=R (views equal revenues) platform means that you've been receiving significant payouts for your article and we wish for your continued success. As a friendly reminder, the contract you digitally signed also states that in order to continue receiving those payments, you must remain in good standing with our company and in order to remain in good standing, you will cooperate with any criminal or civil investigation that results from the publication of your work. I understand that the nature of your story is such that the anonyminty of your sources is critical, but remember that you are representing not just your integrity, but the integrity of the Reviled Media Network. I'd be happy to discuss this matter farther at a mutually agreed-upon time. My personal cell number is XXX-XXX-XXXX.

Sincerely,

Scotty

Scott Lim

President and CEO

Reviled Media Networks

From: ELLE@abyssus.net "ELLE Unknown"

To: DDennis@reviledmag.com "David Dennis"

Subject: FW: Police Investigation Protocol

Date: 9.26.XX at 09:18pm

Your boss is a real asshole. Does he not use spellcheck? Is he a grown man? Is he really your boss?

ELLE

PS. I heard they found Buster Brown trying to book a private, one-way flight to Toronto. I love that he's too sophisticated to hoof it down to Mexico like a respectable American criminal. I also heard that he was a real mess. He has apparently been self-mutilating; slashes all over his body, even his face. That sound like the normal behavior of a newly-married millionaire to you?

From: DaVeD@abyssus.net

To: ELLE@abyssus.net "ELLE Unknown"

Subject: Asshole Scott

Date: 9.27.XX at 10:20pm

Elle,

That's not even the worst of it. He doesn't use spellcheck because he watched a FredTalk called "Spellcheck is for Pussies". He forwarded it to all the magazine staff like we a) give a shit and b) would agree with such an assessment. The video instead suggested you get a woman to read your work and correct it for you, because "that's just one small way for men to re-assert their dominance in this backwards feminist era". Tip-of-the-shit-iceberg. And if you're wondering, yes, he's named in several sexual harassment lawsuits.

Anyway, I got an Abyssus account because I wanted to talk to you more without leaving a trail at work. Since they caught Buster Brown (full disclosure: I had to look that reference up, and no, I didn't hear about Cay being all cut up – how did you know about it and that he did it to himself?) things have calmed down a lot. Now we're debating if we should run what promises to be a sterling piece of journalism called, "Around the World in Eighty BJ's". You can guess who is in full support of it and will likely accept it, despite my many misgivings.

I'll be in touch.

Dave

From: DaVeD@abyssus.net

To: ELLE@abyssus.net "ELLE Unknown"

Subject: Re: Asshole Scott

Date: 9.28.XX at 12:34am

How did you know Kelsey Castleton was eating cat entrails? I can't stop thinking about that. You made that up right? Cause you don't like her or Cay or something? I've read like fifty-seven (no exaggeration) different news reports about the recovery of her body and nothing mentions that. Again, you don't have to disclose your sources but… the fuck, dude? I also read (on /r/AnchoriteCity) that she had drugs in her system that weren't there for the first autopsy. At first I thought it was odd that she had an autopsy but I guess when you're 27 and in perfect health and keel over out of nowhere from heart failure, people ask questions. And then, if after all that you show up in some shithole tenement building looking for all the world like you've been alive or animated or some shit for the last month, people gotta find answers somewhere, right?

Dave

From: DaVeD@abyssus.net

To: ELLE@abyssus.net "ELLE Unknown"

Subject: Re: Re: Asshole Scott

Date: 9.28.XX at 2:46am

Two of the resurrected, Leni Verlis and Rachelle Emerson also died of 'natural causes', at 31 and 34, respectively. All married within the last year to some scumbag golden boy. Martin Verlis and Rich Emerson made their millions on Wall Street, but Leni and Rachelle's ties ran deep here. I went to high school with Rachelle, she was a year ahead of me. She was homecoming queen. I heard she skipped two grades in middle school. We weren't friends or anything, but I knew her. In your article you mentioned that Leni's family owned a lot of real estate around here, and they do, but her mom personally ran that little Turkish café downtown. So I knew her, too. I tried to go in there this past weekend but it's still closed. Sucks, because it was one of my favorite spots to hangout. Leni and her family weren't just like, dickbag gentrifiers preying on the poor. They meant a lot to a lot of people. I'm guessing you're not from around here originally, but people in the AC don't have much to be proud of. We're just a shitty little crime-ridden city at the edge of Cleveland with a high rate of sex trafficking and methamphetamine addiction. This place sucks. But we were proud of those girls. I really wish I'd pulled your story.

From: DaVeD@abyssus.net

To: ELLE@abyssus.net "ELLE Unknown"

Subject: Re: Re: Asshole Scott

Date: 9.28.XX at 4:12am

I'm trying to say that these were real people and shit like this just doesn't happen to real people. maybe I'm a 'normie' ('normy'?), but this is just some super fucked up shit and it's making me super uncomfortable. I appreciate your kind words in your previous message about being afraid of this 'Priest of Breathing' person, but I'm really starting to wonder about your 'methods' and your angle. you came highly recommended. Your clips were impevcable. How do you know shit cops don't even know?

From: ELLE@abyssus.net "ELLE Unknown"

To: DaVeD@abyssus.net

Subject: Re: Re: Re: Asshole Scott

Date: 9.28.XX at 4:32am

David,

Get some sleep. Stop while you're ahead. You don't want any part of this. Trust me.

ELLE

From: DaVeD@abyssus.net

To: ELLE@abyssus.net "ELLE Unknown"

Subject: Re: Re: Re: Re: Asshole Scott

Date: 9.28.XX at 7:39am

i can't sleep. Please just tell me what you know. I knew rachelle. I wrote her a poem. I liked her. She wasn't into me but she wasn't a bitch about it like most girls are. I just want to know if someone hurt her. Like before she died.

From: ELLE@abyssus.net "ELLE Unknown"

To: DaVeD@abyssus.net

Subject: Re: Re: Re: Re: Re: Asshole Scott

Date: 9.28.XX at 5:49pm

David,

You have to get yourself together. If someone did hurt her before she died, what exactly are you of all people going to do about it? That is what I have been trying to tell you. Perhaps I have been too oblique so let me make it clear: stay the fuck away from this story. Stay the fuck away from Kedger's Point. And stay the fuck away from me.

ELLE

From: ELLE@abyssus.net "ELLE Unknown"

To: DaVeD@abyssus.net

Subject: A Compromise

Date: 9.30.XX at 8:02am

David,

You seem like a stupid, impetuous person and since I have not heard anything from you in two days I would like to present you with an offer: I will tell you everything I know (sans sources) if you promise to stay away from this story. I will tell you what (as far as I understand) happened to Kelsey Castleton, Leni Verlis, and Rachelle Emerson. You have to promise me that you will not try to follow up on this. I hate to do this but as insurance, if you attempt to further investigate any aspect of this story, I will let everyone at Reviled Mag, the Anchorite College alumni association, your parents (Steven Dennis SSN XX2-8X-90XX, Maureen Dennis SSN XX5-3X-27XX), brother (Christopher Dennis-Harland SSN XX9-5X-55XX), brother-in-law (Jon Dennis-Harland SSN XX1-4X-04XX), and the entire internet, see the video I recorded via your webcam of you... vigorously watching hair porn on September 26th from 11:31pm to 11:43pm. I do not want to do this. I really don't. But I do not know any other way to keep you safe. I can defend myself in so many ways but you can't even be bothered to put a piece of tape over your webcam while jerking off.

Obviously, I did not know that you personally knew any of the women involved. And I apparently cannot help but drop a juicy little detail whenever I get the chance. It is a problem. If we had had this conversation via your work's email account, I could have just deleted our correspondence remotely. Abyssus is impenetrable, so I am fucked. And it isn't like you'll just forget anyway. Look just please respond as soon as you get this message. I'm sure you'll be upset but I am doing this to protect you.

I don't know why either.

ELLE

PS. I am including an excerpt of the video (just fifteen seconds) so you'll know I am serious.

Attachments: DaveDMovie.mov

From: DaVeD@abyssus.net

To: ELLE@abyssus.net "ELLE Unknown"

Subject: Re: A Compromise

Date: 9.30.XX at 8:12am

You crazy hacker baitch. What the fuck? Delete that shit now or I'll call the police. You're harrassing me. Fuck!

Fuck. Fuck. Okay, I won't do anything else. Please. Please don't show that to anyone. Fuck.

Fuck I'm not even at work yet. Fuck. Please don't show that to anyone. I went to Kedger's Point this weekend. I saw some scary shit. Please don't show that video to anyone. PLEASE! We can talk if you want. I will tell you what I saw.

Please. Please. Please don't show that to anyone.

Dave

From: ELLE@abyssus.net "ELLE Unknown"

To: DaVeD@abyssus.net

Subject: Re: Re: A Compromise

Date: 9.30.XX at 9:12am

David,

I think you are the dumbest person I have ever not met. What the fuck do you mean, you "went to Kedger's Point"? Are you insane?

You're off work by 6pm, right? Download the WHOSAT app to your pc (NOT YOUR PHONE) as soon as you get home. Create an account with your Abyssus email address. At 7:30pm you'll receive a message.

ELLE

WHOSAT Application v4.5

BEGIN CHAT TRANSCRIPT

September 30th, 20XX 7:30pm – 9:12pm

ELLE: Hey

DaVeD: Yeah hi

DaVeD: What the fuck, Elle.

ELLE: I know. I'm trying to protect you. I was, at least.

DaVeD: Thanks. I can't believe you recorded me.

ELLE: I can't believe you leave that camera wide open on your computer. Left. Good on you for finally taping it shut.

DaVeD: Jesus, did you just check again? You know what, I don't even want to know. Fuck.

ELLE: Tell me what happened at Kedger's Point.

DaVeD: Tell me what happened to Rachelle.

ELLE: You aren't in much position to tell me what to do, David. Not to be a dick about it, but… c'mon man.

DaVeD: I don't even care about the video anymore. I just want to know what happened to her. Maybe it'll help me make sense of the fucked up shit I saw. Maybe.

ELLE: WHAT DID YOU SEE?

DaVeD: Why haven't you been out there? Seen it for yourself, Little Miss Hacker?

ELLE: Because I'm not a fucking idiot. That place... isn't safe. To put it mildly.

DaVeD: That's true. I saw... do you know what a 'shade' is?

ELLE: Like, something that blocks light?

DaVeD: No, like in mythology, I guess.

ELLE: Like the spirit of a dead person?

DaVeD: Yeah. That's what I saw. I saw shades.

DaVeD: At least seven of them. That's the best way I can describe them.

DaVeD: But they were solid. Physical. Like the faded versions of the people they used to be. They were like...strung out. And that place and the people smelled...I threw up. Twice. Gagged all the way back home.

ELLE: Can you start from the beginning?

DaVeD: I went there Saturday morning. Early.

ELLE: Did you have any weapons with you or anything?

DaVeD: What kind of weapon would I have?

ELLE: Like a gun or something? You're the white boy, don't they give you an assault rifle at birth?

DaVeD: Very funny.

ELLE: Go on. I can't believe you just walked your happy ass down there…

DaVeD: It seemed deserted at first. I took the bus. I was alone. The closest stop was like six blocks from the place so I had a nice walk through what I can only describe as AC's own version of Tartarus.

ELLE: Sometimes I forget that you majored in Classics but you always find a way to remind me.

DaVeD: You're a fucking creep. Anyway, I got to the building and… it was like… being in a warzone. Except the war had ended a long time ago. The place is uninhabitable. I'm talking windows blasted out of their casings, broken glass fucking everywhere, no vegetation, half the telephone wires were just cut in half and dangling in the streets. Dude I even saw those big rusty drums sitting on a corner with fires lit inside them. I've only seen that shit in the movies. It was crazy. I saw a wrapper for 'Mr. Chuckies Burgers and Brew'. Mr. Chuckies went out of business like 12 years ago. Time had stopped there.

DaVeD: Anyway, there's a courtyard and there was this hollow-eyed cadaverous-looking dude just sitting on the steps that lead back into the entryway into the building proper. I thought he was going to say something to me but I walked passed him and he didn't even fucking blink. He didn't move. And he'd shit himself. He was just sitting in it. That's the first time I threw up.

ELLE: Gross

DaVeD: It gets way worse. His fingernails were like… at least five, maybe six inches long I thought… okay it sounds weird but I thought he was holding like, a bunch of strawberries or something. But I got closer and he was digging. Into himself. He had gouged out parts of his chest and upper arms.

ELLE: Fuck me.

DaVeD: He was staring out past me, past the courtyard, like he was staring right out of this fucking world and into somewhere else. I'll never forget what it felt like to realize what he was doing. I felt like I had fallen into someplace. Truth be told, I still feel like I'm there.

ELLE: I bet.

DaVeD: After walking past him I was in the entryway and it was all dark. I mean, there was a little light seeping from the exit at the other end, but it was mostly dark. Caliginous, even. On either side of the hall were the doors to the apartments. They were all closed. I walked until I came to a stairwell.

DaVeD: The second floor was… unbelievable. It was darker because there was no light from an open exit like there was downstairs. And there were more 'people' in the halls. A woman, I think, was sitting up against the wall at the top of the stairs. At first I could only see her body (she'd soiled herself too) and as I stepped up more and more of her was revealed. She was making like a chewing, gristly noise.

ELLE: Oh fuck you David.

DaVeD: No, you have to hear all of it. I have to tell somebody. You were right. You were fucking right and I never should have gone out there. But you owe me. So now you listen. Read. Whatever.

DaVeD: I saw her face. What was left of it. There was just… rawness and redness and a row of red-stained teeth. She had chewed off her whole lower lip. She was chewing automatically. You could tell, her movements were… mechanistic. Her arms were wrapped around herself, like she'd been cold once but had forgotten to care. There was caked blood and filth all over her. And she was staring out of the world just like that dude downstairs.

ELLE: How the fuck did you not leave after that?!

DaVeD: I screamed. Fuck it, I screamed like a girl. Anyone would have, shit. She didn't move. Didn't blink. She was gone. Everybody in that place was like that.

ELLE: How many people were there?

DaVeD: I saw seven 'people'. I think there were more, but their doors were locked. Some of them weren't. There were animal parts lying around. Carcasses chewed down to the bones. There was maybe what looked like a scalp at the far end of the hallway. Just a scalp, lying on the dirty floor.

ELLE: Fuck that. Fuck that to hell.

ELLE: Did you call the police?

DaVeD: What the fuck are the police going to do, Elle? They'd already been there!

ELLE: No, I mean, they couldn't have seen that. Kedger's Point has been condemned for years. And the reports said all the other apartments had been abandoned. The fucking building is condemned.

DaVeD: What reports?

ELLE: The internal police reports.

DaVeD: That's how you knew what happened to Kelsey and Leni and Rachelle. You hacked the police records.

ELLE: It doesn't matter, but I feel obligated to tell you that nobody says 'hacked' anymore.

DaVeD: Thanks for the tip. What else do you know?

ELLE: Let me ask you one more question and then I'll tell you everything.

DaVeD: What?

ELLE: What was in Kelsey's apartment?

DaVeD: Nothing. I mean, some shitty furniture and garbage. And a checkered blotter.

ELLE: A what?

DaVeD: Like blotting paper? For acid? There was a sheet underneath the bed. I thought it was just trash but the pattern caught my eye.

ELLE: What pattern?

DaVeD: I took a picture. I took lots of pictures actually.

ELLE: Why the fuck did… never mind.

DaVeD:

KPblotter.jpg

ELLE: How'd you know it was a blotter?

DaVeD: I grew up here and there ain't much for the youth to do, so… hallucinogens.

ELLE: It's here now. I mean that's obvious but I didn't have all the pieces. I do now.

DaVeD: What? You lost me.

ELLE: I've been looking into this shit for… decades. Chasing the myth. Stalking the rumors. Wait, before I tell you what I know, what happened after you left Kelsey's apartment?

DaVeD: Nothing. I mean I just left. That hollowed-out guy said something to me. Or he said something out loud while I was running the fuck away.

ELLE: What did he say?

DaVeD: It sounded like, "My voice is dead" or "My voice is dying" or something.

ELLE: "Song of my soul, my voice is dead." Please don't ever go back there and if you ever seen that man or that woman again or anyone else from that place you run from them. Do you understand me? I'm not kidding, David.

DaVeD: Why the fuck will I ever see them again? After this shit I'll probably never leave my house.

ELLE: Good.

DaVeD: How did you know what he said? Why does it sound familiar?

ELLE: Because it's from R.W. Chambers' story, "The King in Yellow". It's a fictionalized, ruinous city that exists in another dimension. It's a mythos, like the Cthulhu stories, and all kinds of writers have played around with the concept.

DaVeD: So...

ELLE: Somebody, we'll call him the Priest of Breathing, made a drug that takes its users to Carcosa. Hence the name, Carcosine.

DaVeD: I don't understand.

ELLE: Yeah well there's a lot I'm pretty fucking baffled about too, but that's what I know.

DaVeD: So, that's how those girls came back? Is that what you're saying?

ELLE: Yes. I know it doesn't make any kind of sense. That's the thing about this whole fucking story. The more I chase after it the more it unravels. I'm tired, David.

DaVeD: Do you want to talk more later? It is late.

ELLE: I mean I'm tired of this. I'm tired of hunting this shit. I'm tired of living like this.

DaVeD: How do you mean?

DaVeD: ELLE?

DaVeD: Fuck did you leave?

ELLE: No, I'm still here. Always fucking here. The spider's in her web, watching everything. Look at that pattern in the blotter. Tell me where it ends and where it begins.

DaVeD: I've seen some really fucked up shit the last few days. Some weird optical illusion is the least of my concerns right now.

ELLE: Good. That's good actually.

DaVeD: How do you mean? Hang on, my phone just made a weird noise.

ELLE: I deleted the image from your phone and hard drive.

DaVeD: WHAT THE FUCK ELL GODDAMMIT

ELLE: You don't need it for anything. To keep staring at it, like I have, for as long as I have… it'll just start to tempt you.

DaVeD: Could you stop fucking with my devices? Goddamn.

ELLE: I will. Carcosine makes the living feel dead and the dead feel alive. But their appetites change.

DaVeD: What are you fucking saying?

ELLE: You said it yourself, you saw 'shades'. You were more correct than you thought.

DaVeD: I was just using that as a description. Are you serious? Those people were really dead?

ELLE: No, those people were alive and they now think they are dead. Somebody, I'm guessing the Priest of Breathing or one of his… servants, cleared those people out when the cops came. And once they left, they brought them back. Kind of them, really. Leni and Kelsey and Rachelle, those women were dead. Their bodies killed them. And their grieving husband's found something to make them seem as if they were alive. And they came back, but they came back wrong. They always come back wrong. You cannot invert the pattern.

DaVeD: Where are you? I know you're in town but where exactly? I don't like what you're saying

ELLE: You couldn't find me even if you really tried. That's sweet though. I have some, you know? From a long time ago. I've been saving it.

DaVeD: Please don't do anything stupid.

ELLE: I think, maybe, being alive is the stupidest thing any of us will ever do. To keep at it, like somehow things will right themselves.

DaVeD: You don't have to go all edgelord on me, okay? We can talk about this some more. I can meet you somewhere. Anywhere.

ELLE: That's nice. I thought you were mad at me?

DaVeD: Okay, yeah I am but… this is freaking me the fuck out. Hard. And I don't like what you're saying.

ELLE: I don't like what I'm saying. I don't like what I know. You know how earlier you said that you'll never forget the faces of the people in Kedger's Point? That faraway look in their eyes?

DaVeD: Yeah, so?

ELLE: When you climax in that video, you had the same look on your face. We all do. Death is peace, David. Peace is death. It may look ugly on the outside, but inside, it's the only thing that calms us. That focal point of bright black at the center of everything. Maybe what the Priest of Breathing is doing is a good thing.

DaVeD: Jesus Elle. Please don't do whatever it is you're going to do.

ELLE: You know exactly what I'm going to do. Maybe someday we'll meet face to face.

DaVeD: Shit we could meet nnow! Please! None no one else will believe this shit!

ELLE: In dim Carcosa. Bye David.

DaVeD: Elle?

ELLE: User ELLE is no longer connected.

DaVeD: Elle?

DaVeD: What the fuck? Elle?

END CHAT TRANSCRIPT

Paula's Afterword

"I saw an X. No matter how I turned it, inverted it, reversed it, there was always the 'X' blaring at me in clear black and white. I saw gradations too, pixelated shimmers of non-colours in the corners of my eyes. 'X marks the spot', came to mind. 'That's terribly cliché' soon followed. I wondered what would happen if I stared into the points of transition in the image, zoomed in until the binary blurred. I saw an X. "Exile in Extremis" was inspired by R.W. Chambers' The King in Yellow and Gemma Files' and Stephen J. Barringer's 'each thing i show you is a piece of my death'."

THE PRICKLES

KIT POWER

Staring at the picture was giving him The Prickles.

More of a tingle, at first. Like a tickle, but... not. It was at once more delicate and more profound. It started in the centre of his scalp. Then it would spread out in a circle, like water running over his head, only not cold, but warm and, well, prickly.

The Prickles.

He remembers...

he is less than five years old, and all perspectives are huge, the world outsized, giant, not built for him, and he has nightmares where he is high up in the ceiling of a train station and the railings that are supposed to keep him safe are spread too far apart, built to keep giants safe, but not him, and in his dreams he feels dizzy and knows he will fall between those gaping gaps and onto the platform far below, and at some point, some time, at this age, he passes a huge corrugated shed, and from inside comes the whining of a saw in wood, high and loud, a painful whine/wailing noise, grinding, shrieking, and the smell of fresh wood shavings mingles with the look of the corrugated iron, and that in turn evokes the inside of celery, and all of a sudden the bitter taste of celery floods his young mouth, mixed with the smell of fresh sawdust and the whine of the blade that he cannot see and does not know of, and the cold, somehow harsh quality of the corrugated iron, and that night, on the edge of sleep, remembering these sensations, feeling them collide and circle each other in his memory, like pieces of a jigsaw puzzle that do not really fit but somehow seem in each component piece like they must make a picture, he gets The Prickles and he also recalls

he is taken by his mother to the shoe shop, to be measured up for new smart black shoes, and though he either does not know or does not remember, they are school shoes, his first pair, and this is a rite of passage, the moment where childhood moves from something basically free to something basically regimented, controlled, but for now he's in the shoe shop, and the nice lady has put his foot in the measuring device and slid the deliciously cool metal against his toes and the side of his feet, and then she has gone and come back with a box that contains the black shoes, and as he puts them on, she's knelt down and leaning forward, and her fingers push into the leather, to check the fit around his toes, and as soon as she does, whoosh! The Prickles burst over his head, and he feels like his ears must be glowing, and the sensation is delicious, and he barely hears the nice lady commenting on the fit, because he's practically shivering with delight, and he wants to get a new pair of shoes every week just so that he can feel this, but he knows he can't because his mother tells him often enough that she is not made of bloody money

and then he remembers

the vicar at the church where he sings in the choir, and the father of the first girl he'll kiss, and how his favourite part is not the singing, not the hymns, nor the prayers (though he remembers finding the corpse of a fly, perfectly intact, under the wooden railing where they take communion, and how he'd taken it and secreted it under a kneeling cushion in the choir benches, and how when the prayers came he'd sometimes take it out and gently stroke its head, feeling, or imagining he could feel, the short hairs there, and thinking of nothing much but feeling at peace and like he was expressing love, somehow), nor even the brown envelope at the end of every month that would contain the silver and copper he was paid for his duties, but rather the moment in each service when he would go to the altar to receive his blessing - not communion, he was too young for that, though he envied the older parishioners the sip of wine, and most of all the sweet-looking wafer, the flavour of which was a source of fevered speculation, though he'd outgrow the faith long before he was of age to partake, and would go to his end having never tasted the Communion Bread - and he'd kneel at the polished wooden railing, and the priest would say a blessing and touch the top of his head, lightly, and woosh! The Prickles, right down to the back of his neck, and it would fill him with pleasure, but gradually, with the blessings, The Prickles began to fade, and he told his mother, and his mother said he should tell the vicar, but he thought deep down that the problem was him, not the priest, so he said nothing, and then one day the vicar announced he could no longer be their vicar, because he did not believe his church should allow women to be priests, and then he left the church and the village, and the boy stopped going

and that leads him to remember

the man he now thinks of as 'The Ghost', but who then he called teacher and brother, is talking to him about the light and the dark, and the boy, who is now a teenager on the way to manhood, talks longingly of the dark, employing the poetry that sounds so powerful to the ears of the young and so predictable and twee to the ears of the old, and as he waxes lyrical, he utters the phrase 'wondrous savagery' and immediately The Ghost says 'remove your shirt', and he does so, confused, but not nervous, and The Ghost says, 'turn around' and he does so, sitting on the edge of his bed with his back to The Ghost. And The Ghost places an ancient spearhead he has seen before on The Ghost's altar into his chest - the point dimples his flesh, just shy of a scratch, The Ghost's touch is sure, and all at once, The Prickles start a wave from the centre of his scalp that bloom out as The Ghost moves the point of the spear down his chest in a straight line towards his stomach, and he breathes slow and he feels calm but he is alive to everything, in that moment, and The Prickles have him good, and afterward he's told it was A Test and he Passed, and he believes it, but he wonders

and before he knows it

he's watching the husband of a work colleague taking a screwdriver to the guts of his new PC, with a roll-up dangling from the corner of his mouth as he waffles about Captain Beefheart and Syd Barrett-era Floyd, and he should be at least concerned, because he's spent all this money on a processor and motherboard and additional RAM and a really groovy graphics card and now none of it is working properly and it's too much money to write off but the PC shop won't take returned components, on the basis that if you buy them you're supposed to know what you're fucking doing, and he thought he had, but it turned out he really, really hadn't, and when he'd been bemoaning his situation in the open plan and his colleague had said 'oh, my husband's really good at that kind of thing, I'm sure he can help', he'd taken her up on it like a flash, and her husband looks to him like a sparkie or a chippie, and he'd had plenty of time to regret the hasty, desperate decision, especially as the guy is smoking in a non-smoking rented house and drinking wine out of one of his chunky squash glasses, but once her husband takes the back off of the computer and gently starts touching the components, all at once The Prickles starts up and he knows he's okay, the guy knows what he's doing, and sure enough, though it takes him a further twenty minutes of fucking about, he gets the machine up and running, and the crooked smile he shoots when Windows boots up is beautiful

he's completely lost now, recollections pinballing into each other, and he sees

his friend - not a friend he's been good to, but a friend who's been good to him - a friend who has discovered weed, and embraced it like a lover, and he sees himself, in an outbuilding at his friend's farm, and his friend is building a joint, his long artistic fingers manipulating the tobacco and the grass and the paper with skill and delicacy and finesse, and sure, he's feeling pretty stoned, but The Prickles are nothing like that, they are something else, and he feels them like a wave, as he watches his talented friend employed with dedication and love in his new creative endeavour, treating the joint-manufacturing like sculpture, like a holy calling, and his face splits in a smile, and he laughs, and says 'You're like that old dude in the advert making his cricket bat' and he giggles at the thought, and it might have sounded mocking but he meant it deep and sincere, it was a sincere expression of love for the friend who he'd not treated well but who had treated him well, and the laugh is a laugh of affection, and

then there's

the friend he's been good to, who has not been good to him, and will become not-a-friend before their time is through, but right now he's at or around his lowest ebb and the not-friend can see, and buys him a drink, because not-friend has a job and he does not, and after enduring his misery for as long as the not-friend can (which is not, truth to tell, very long, patience not being a huge part of not-friend's general makeup), not-friend finally says to him 'You have to take the ring off', and he shakes his head, and says he can't, and not-friend shakes his head and says, quietly but firmly, 'I'll hold it for you, I will keep it safe' (this turns out to be a lie, though neither of them know it, and by the time the lie is revealed, it will no longer matter), 'but you have to take it off, because it's not around your finger, it's around your neck' and just like that, he feels The Prickles, recognising the ring (ha) of truth, and he nods and hands over the ring and immediately a huge weight lifts and he realises he had stopped seeing a future, and suddenly now he can again, and he blinks away tears of relief

and then he thinks

about visiting his mother, because there are too many women in his life and not nearly enough time, and he's suddenly realised that he might, in fact, have met The One, and she sits him down, calm and without judgement, and they complete a tarot, and two of the cards from the Arthurian deck she favours at the time will haunt him, and the second of those cards is The Wounded King, which appears inverted, meaning that it is important to cast away the image of the legendary hero that sleeps under the hill, awaiting the bugle call to rescue the world, that this is a facade, a distraction, a lie told to himself to prevent and foreclose effort, striving, to slumber and avoid the responsibility and joy and pain and risk and reward of being alive and present in the fucking world and trying and striving and yeah, sure, failing, because success is what happens if you fail enough times and don't give up, and it haunts him, right to his end it follows him, causing him always to wonder if he's making excuses, using that mind of his to rationalise doing less than he could, being less than he should, it haunts him, but he forgets the first card, the one that confirms the question, the moment when he turns over The Lovers and The Prickles run down him and he knows and he looks at the picture, and he thinks, what is this feeling? And he thinks, why is this feeling? And he marvels, at both the fact of The Prickles and their inexplicable nature.

He marvels.

Postscript: He's forgotten all of this and more, when he's standing at the site of what he hopes will be an open air gig - the first for his band - and the sparkie listens carefully to what he's planning and how he's planning it, and after he's asked a couple of questions the sparkie turns toward the main building, hands on his hips, and he squints, and The Prickles hit our man, and he smiles to himself, and he thinks 'Okay, that's okay, this guy clearly knows what he's fucking doing, we'll be fine', and the moment is there and gone, and he never remembers it, and he never forgets it.

Kit's Afterword

"I stared at it a lot. I kept seeing a tunnel, and maybe a falling sensation - the transition from death to life? Ah, but hasn't that been done to death and back? :) So I took a mental step back, examined the contours, the perimeter. Spikes. That's what I kept coming back to. That seemed more important than the tunnel, somehow, but Spikes, like Tunnel, isn't actually a story.

"Then, I actually started getting The Prickles - precisely as I describe them in the opening paragraphs.

"I don't know what they mean, any more than Tunnel and Spikes, but I realised they were a way in, a way to tell a story, a life story, disparate events linked by a shared, inexplicable sensation.

"I wrote the draft in one sitting over two hours, and went back and edited only very lightly. It's quite a feeling, when the words flow that easy."

THE JAZZIVERSE

JONATHAN BUTCHER

Trumpets, drums, and saxophones exploded from the lounge's two huge speakers, like musical warfare.

Bending forwards in his armchair, Dad squinted at the work-in-progress lying across his lap: a black-and-white ink design so intricate that it almost hurt to look at. He stroked another dark line into the corner of the eye-boggling pattern.

"That could be one of your best, Dad," I said, watching him from the couch. "I can't even work out how you've done it."

I was visiting home for the first time in months, after an email from Dad saying he was missing our infrequent games of pool. I lived a couple of hundred miles away, and since his heart attack a few years back he no longer travelled.

He laughed. "I don't know where these bloody designs come from either, son. I just experiment – it's the jazz in me! Speaking of jazz, listen to these two solos."

A piano plinky-dinked into the room, poking its head out from a flat note here and a seemingly random chord there. Seconds later the brass instruments and piano paused, letting the lone drummer slam the skins like a man deranged. His technique was impeccable: a whirlwind of polyrhythms, ever-changing rudiments, and lightning-fast hi-hat work. After a minute or two, the other musicians joined the tune again.

"Okay. I felt that drum solo," I admitted.

"Of course you felt it!" Dad said, reaching to the coffee table, cracking open a can, and pouring amber fluid into his glass tankard. "That was my main man, Buddy Rich! Best drummer that's ever been, and no mistake."

I considered contenders from the worlds of rock and metal – John Bonham, Neil Peart, Hellhammer – but kept my mouth shut.

"I don't get the rest of it, though," I said, as atonal trumpet squeals and erratic time signatures swept through the room. "What am I supposed to be hearing?"

Dad smiled, his wispy hair thin but neatly cropped, his eyes mischievous. His 78-year-old face was simply an older version of my own. "Jazz is the most expressive music there is, sunbeam."

"But how can big band jazz be expressive or emotional? It sounds so unplanned."

"That's what gives it so much feeling, sonny-Jim!" Dad cried. "They're playing from the heart, they're feeling it, right there and then."

To Dad, jazz wasn't just music – it was practically a religion. He'd sold his old LPs a few years back, but he still had hundreds of CDs, DVDs, and hardbacks showcasing the subject. They lined several bookshelves arranged throughout the house, alphabetically ordered and meticulously filed on his ailing-but-functional PC.

From the lounge speakers, the entire band came crashing in for the tune's crescendo: brass players, double bass, drums, and piano. It was an exhilarating cacophony, like a howling thunderstorm, or a party just before it careens out-of-control.

I said, "This part almost reminds me of a piece of black metal – Emperor, or Aborym, or someone."

"That's not music, son. You can't even hear what they're saying, with all that growling and grizzling."

I countered him. "But, like jazz, they harness something that sounds horrible and chaotic, and give what could have sounded like a mess *power*."

"That's not power. That's just screaming ab-dabs."

"Dad, some of them are awesome musicians."

"Bollocks," he said, with a chuckle.

For Dad, if a composition or genre didn't fit his expectations, then no one had the right to compare it to jazz.

The music hammered the living-room walls and I noticed that Dad had lost himself within it. His eyes were pressed shut and his fists thrust into the air, celebratory and violent and deadly serious all at once. Dad was no longer a pensioner as the track approached its finale; he was ageless.

The tune soared and roared like something trying to break free from the stereo, raw and untamed, and for a moment I was almost afraid. The feeling intensified and I began to look around the lounge, filled with the uncanny sense that a presence loomed close by, just out of sight.

Then the track was over.

There was the briefest silence before the recording's enraptured audience bellowed its approval.

"Dad?" I asked. "Did something almost happen just then? It felt weird. Like the music wanted to… get out."

Dad sipped his beer and made a noise of pleasure, like a parched dog lapping from a bowl of water. "Lovely jubbly. Can't beat the first taste of the day."

"Dad."

He blinked. Now, my dad wasn't an untruthful person – he was very much a "what you see is what you get" sort of guy – but in that blink, I saw that he was hiding something.

"I suppose it's about time you knew. I actually asked you to pop back home for a reason." He stood up, his joints clacking like marionettes, and I followed him upstairs to the bedroom. "This stays between you and me, right?"

Dad went to his wardrobe; a tall pine construction that he had worked on when I'd been a boy, perhaps 25 years ago. "Look here." He pointed at the thin dark crack between the wardrobe's rear and the wallpaper.

I peeked, and pulled my head away with a gasp. "What the fuck..."

"Excuse your French," he said.

I leaned forwards again, closer to what should have been a sliver of shadow, but which contained a line of light.

"Help me shift this, son."

"I don't understand."

But I did as he asked, and as we heaved it away, light spilled from an opening that until then had been hidden by the furniture. Dad shuffled sideways towards the narrow beam, and said, "Come on."

Then he vanished.

"Dad?" I asked. "Dad!"

The strip glowed. I put my face to it again, but the luminescence was too great to keep my eyes open. I braced myself and stepped closer.

My guts clenched, as though I'd taken an abrupt fall. The glare became blinding, too intense.

Then I emerged in a nightclub.

More specifically, on the performance stage of a nightclub.

Brightness bore down on me like a searchlight over an escaped prisoner. My ears filled with a near-deafening sound: big band jazz, attacking from all sides. I spun full circle. A guy with vast, bullfrog cheeks blew a trumpet to my right, and a haggard-looking man to my left was playing a sax. A row of trombonists played at the edge of the stage, a fellow in a neat suit with Lego hair played drums, and a gaunt-looking man was at the piano. There was even a fellow with a thin moustache playing electric guitar while smoking a rolled cigarette. Then… Christ… right at the front of the stage, under his own spotlight, I saw my dad blowing a saxophone. He grinned at me as he played, clearly enjoying my confusion and shock.

A microphone stood tall in front of me, but although I knew the tune they were playing I was just too damn flabbergasted to remember any words. As the rest of the band bashed, blew, thrummed, and tapped out the music, I shuffled closer to the mic. The spotlight's intensity lessened enough so I could make out our audience, which drank, smoked, and jived to the jazz that was rocking the stage.

With the microphone in my hand, I closed my eyes, trying to summon some courage. I'd been in bands and was more used to performing rock and metal vocals live, but I could just about sing. No lyrics came to mind, so I readied myself to scat, but then the tune ended with an abrupt final note. I stood there with my mouth hung open and the crowd laughed, as if my forgetting of the words had been part of the show; some kind of visual comedy.

The crowd cried in a single voice: *"BADA-LADA-LO!"*

Afterwards, the adrenaline of the music and the transition from the quiet bedroom into a raucous jazz club overwhelmed me. My temperature plummeted and the shakes rattled through me. I was almost sick onstage.

Dad led me down ten steps to the club floor. He seemed to shake hands with, or at least wink at, every person we passed. Being so comfortably sociable was quite unlike Dad when we were back home.

As we crossed the club I saw how immaculate the other guests looked, with dinner jackets and perfectly-pressed shirts for the men, and tasteful but sensual dresses for the women. I also noticed that the high walls of the club bore no windows but were carved into the impression of different jazz instruments, and pillars carved with elaborate musical notes divided the club floor. A towering grey stone saxophone stood on its curved base in the far corner near the stage, while on the other side of the performance area and just as high, a trumpet pointed up towards the ceiling. On the wall behind the bar, which was where Dad was leading me, there loomed a quartet of enormous stone-carved clarinettists, their sculpted eyes squeezed tight in concentration as they played.

"The usual, Les?" the dapper grey-haired bartender asked.

"Yeah, thanks, and one for the boy," Dad replied. "Want the same? Pint of Doombar?"

"Do you do cocktails?" I asked, feeling jittery.

"Best in the Jazziverse," the bartender said, pouring Dad's pint.

"The… Jazziverse," I said. It sounded like a bad joke. "I'll have a Manhattan, then. Sweet. Go hard on the bourbon."

"Eurgh, more of that foreign muck," Dad said, taking up his frothing tankard.

I turned to him as the bartender fixed my drink. Dad's tight-lipped smile seemed smug.

"Well, go on then," I told him.

"Go on, what?" he asked, glugging his beer.

"Tell me what in Satan's cleft anus is going on."

He raised his eyebrows. The bartender laid my Manhattan on the bar. I downed it in one before asking for another.

"Well son," Dad said. He stretched out his arms and gestured to the wide, tall room. "Welcome to my church. I don't think much about religion or any of that cobblers, but jazz… well, jazz is different."

"Jazz isn't just music," Dad continued. "Why else would I have spent my whole bloody life listening to it?"

"How long have you been coming here?"

"Gawd, you can't ask me that, sonny-Jim. It's hard to measure the years, once you retire."

"A while though?" I asked, but we were interrupted.

"Hiya, Les!" said a good-looking younger guy with slick dark hair wearing a tight white t-shirt. He held a trumpet in one hand and I felt like I recognised him.

"Hey there, Chet," Dad replied amicably, patting him on the shoulder.

"Great playing tonight. You were really nailing those high notes."

"Ah, you crawler!" Dad laughed.

The young guy slapped Dad on the back without even giving me a glance and headed off into the crowd.

"And stay off that white powder!" Dad called after him.

I shivered. "I can't have, but I felt like I recognised him."

"That, son, was Chet Baker. In the flesh."

"Before…"

Dad's face fell a little. "Before the drugs ruined him, yes."

I felt more disoriented than ever and looked around the bustling club, suddenly recognising faces from my dad's music collection.

Further down the bar there was Woody Herman, waving his clarinet in the air for emphasis. He was telling an anecdote to a circle of guys in black dinner jackets and ladies in glittering dresses.

At a table near the stage, I spotted Cab Calloway sat with Dizzy Gillespie. They sipped drinks and talked but appeared to be staring each other down.

Uproarious cackles exploded behind me, and when I turned I saw Dinah Washington and Ella Fitzgerald. Their arms were linked and they were clutching their stomachs with their free hands, crippled with laughter.

In the corner, surrounded by a group of stocky fellows in suits, was big Frankie: Frank Si-fucking-natra. He caught my eye and winked.

"This place is insane," I told Dad, who was ordering another beer.

"It certainly is, sonny. If it gets too much for you, you can just slip through that door over there and you'll be back home again." He pointed towards a portal marked by a green "EXIT" sign, standing to the left of the unlit stage.

"But what is this place?"

Dad shrugged. "I'm just here to play sax and worship at the altar of jazz, baby!"

"But how the hell is any of this possible? And when did you start playing the sax?"

"We'll talk in a bit – looks like it's time for the second set."

The band members were taking their seats on stage again, and Dad was rushing back to his spot. He walked faster and with surer feet here, in the ridiculously-named Jazziverse – so much so that I hardly recognised him as he paced away.

Moments later, the hum of conversation fell in volume, like a congregation awaiting the words of the preacher. All at once, everyone in the room cried out in perfect unison: *"BADA-LADA-LO!"*

Then came the raucous blare of the band.

I surveyed the room, populated by band members of the distant, colourful past. No one was paying me the slightest interest, which was perhaps unsurprising. There was head-spinning, attention-swallowing jazz being played, and everyone aside from my dad and the bartender seemed to be musical maestros dressed to the 9s. I was just a guy in jeans and a horror movie t-shirt, looking confused.

A little way down, an overweight man with grey hair and a scruffy, unbuttoned brown jacket leaned back against the bar. I vaguely recognised him and headed his way.

"How's it going?" I asked, attempting to copy the guy's casual lean.

He looked at me and wrinkled his nose. "Hi there! Maynard Ferguson," he said, pumping my hand.

"I can't believe this place," I told him. "Do you know my dad?"

I pointed to my father up on stage, who was now blowing his sax: a slim figure who leaned slightly forwards in the "real world", but who was animated and wild here in the Jazziverse, throwing his head back and bending his knees whenever he hit a high note.

Maynard grinned. "Of course I do! We all do. That's the Rev!"

"The Rev?"

"You said it, brother."

"Why'd you call him that?"

Maynard frowned. "Where you been hidin'? The Rev's a prophet, at this big ol' cathedral o' jazz."

"I don't understand," I said. "So, what was that *BADA-LADA-LO* about, then? It was almost like... I don't know... like they were saying *Amen*."

Maynard screwed up his nose again. "Why don't you just enjoy the music, and have another drink? Hey, bartender! Another one o' whatever this nosy parker's havin'!"

"Just an Appletise, thanks," I called, and the bartender delivered the green bottle into my hand with a grin.

When I turned back, Maynard was still looking at me but was now speaking into the ear of a young, Italian-looking guy, who might have been the drummer Louie Bellson.

All these jazz greats from different times in their careers, all looking and playing their best.

I made my way through the tables and past the stage as the first track ended with an explosion of trumpets.

"*BADA-LADA-LO!*" the audience – no, the *congregation* – yelled.

Dad stepped towards the mic. "This one's for you, sonny Jim!"

The drummer and pianist began to play Dave Brubeck's "Take 5", one of the first jazz tracks to be written in a 5/4 timing. A few bars in, Dad started an extra-smooth rendition of the track's famous saxophone section. I stood there mesmerised as the spotlights focused on him, bemused by the idea of one of my family members actually looking cool. I turned to the audience, wondering how many of them were thinking the same.

They were glaring at me – all of them.

Rows and rows of classic jazz gods and goddesses snapped their necks back to focus on my dad, but I'd seen it. I'd expected looks of awe and joy as my father performed, but the whole room had been ignoring the solo saxophonist on stage and glowering in my direction. Now they were watching the band again.

I had a sudden need to reach the door marked with the green "EXIT" sign.

I headed to the side of the stage. None of this felt right and none of it made sense, and I knew, just knew, that when I reached the door it was going to be locked.

I tried the long-bar emergency escape handle.

It didn't even budge.

Brubeck's subtly genius "Take 5" ended and made way for a Kenton-style rendition of "Peanut Vendor". I turned around, feeling the room teeter. The sheer unreality of what was happening hit me like a crash of cymbals, and as I surveyed the crowd – a multicultural, multigenerational swathe of dancing, bopping figures – my vision warped.

I saw something else; something beneath the facade.

These were not the big band leaders, the talented composers, and the musical prodigies of yesteryear. Their faces and outfits were just for show. Beneath the coats of apparent skin and muscle there were eyes without substance, undefined intentions, and expectation – *so much expectation.*

Just as I had when I'd sat in the lounge back in the "real world", as the band played I felt the anticipation of approach, and an absence waiting to be filled. The nightclub, with its red glows, blinking spotlights, and unlikely patrons, was not a space for socialising and musical appreciation – it was really a place of worship.

More than that: it was a place of summoning.

The stage was the parapet, the audience the congregation, and my father, standing up there and playing an instrument that until tonight I'd had no idea he knew how to play, was the preacher.

The Rev.

This wasn't a concert; it was a ritual.

I raced up onto the stage. No one stopped me as I went to the microphone. "Stop! Stop playing, Dad! They're tricking you!"

The musicians halted.

Dad dropped the saxophone with a *clunk*. He watched me in a way I wasn't used to: confident, authoritative, and almost smug.

"You plonker, son." He shook his head and beamed a sudden smile. "No one's tricking me to be here. This is the best bloody bar I've ever known! It's better than The Dog and better than The Lanherne, because while I'm here, I'm surrounded by the greats! If I want to hear Don Ellis performing with Louis Armstrong, I've got it!"

A trumpeter with a bowl haircut and a chin-strap beard waved his hand from the far right of the stage. As he did, a voice that was more like a belch called from the bar, "You tell 'em, big guy!"

Dad said, "If I want the Rat Pack to perform songs by The Beatles, or the Stan Kenton band to play the War of the Worlds album, all I've got to do is ask!"

The audience grew rowdy, whooping at Dad's words.

"BADA-LADA-LO!" people screamed, but no longer in unison; the excitement was now too great for that.

As they bellowed, they changed, soon looking less like a crowd of jazz legends, and more like silhouettes; hungry, hollering shadows.

"But there's something else happening, isn't there, Dad?" I said. "They aren't really who they look like, are they?"

"So what? This is what it's like to feel something *real*!" Dad laughed. "This isn't about a big man with a white beard in the sky; this is jazz, baby, and when we play, we don't mess around!"

"But it's like when we were in the lounge! It's like the music is calling something!"

"Who bloody cares, when the party's this swinging?"

The audience cheered and their shadows swirled, shifting like black mist through the bar. A noxious smell hit my throat and the crowd's pretence was broken. Through the smoky vapours I saw the true form of the revellers: several hundred cloaked figures. Their hoods were lightless, their hands gnarled, parched, and grey. Their faceless shrouds pointed at me, and I knew they weren't jazz musicians.

If I hadn't known better, I'd have said they were cultists.

"What now, then?" I asked, wondering how things had come to this. My dad – my silly, grumpy, eccentric, but very lovable dad – was the band leader to a group of... what? Music worshippers?

Jazz worshippers.

"They always said that I should bring you along, son," Dad said. "I happened to mention that I was missing you living closer by, and that you were in a band, and they got all excited. Said that if you and I played together, nothing could stop us."

"Stop them from *what?*"

"FROM SUMMONING THEM," boomed a third voice. Its tone hummed, like a choir of bees. No figure from the crowd stepped forwards, and the sound seemed to have come from several places at once.

The hooded figures stood or sat motionless in their matching nimbus-grey cloaks. Their frames, their heights, and their postures seemed identical; if they had been in an identity line-up I could not have told them apart.

"YOUR FATHER'S PASSION FOR JAZZ IS POTENT. WE WERE ONCE LEADERS BUT WE HAVE BECOME THE CONGREGATION, AND YOUR FATHER THE REVEREND. HE HAS BROUGHT US CLOSER TO JAZZ-SALVATION."

It was like hundreds of voices speaking together, or perhaps a single voice spoken from hundreds of mouths.

"What do you need me for?" I asked.

"TO PLAY MUSIC ALONG WITH YOUR FATHER, AND TO SUMMON OUR GODS. JAZZ IS A LANGUAGE THAT CALLS… BEYOND."

"He might talk like a wanker, but he's right, son," Dad said from the stage. "Jazz has power. You said it yourself!"

The floor shook with a groaning rumble. I tottered sideways but kept my balance.

"HARK – SOMETHING APPROACHES."

"Who?" I asked.

"THOSE WHO LISTEN. IT IS TIME FOR OUR FINAL PERFORMANCE."

The ground trembled again and the rumble rose to a roar.

"GET TO YOUR PLACES!" the voice commanded. "THEY DEMAND JAZZ!"

The details of what was happening were hazy to me, but there was clearly much at stake. Carried through the walls and from beneath the ground, the sound of whatever the hooded figures were summoning became excruciating: a chorus of howls like a monstrous crowd awaiting a delayed show, impatient and ready to riot.

"NOW!" the voice bellowed.

The hooded figures rushed me, their true appearances merging with that of the jazz musicians they'd pretended to be. The inhuman grey talons that reached from the robes transmuted into fleshy brown or pink hands that grasped my limbs and bustled me towards the stage. I was shoved up the steps and to the front, where the microphone stood like a lone stick figure. I met my dad's eyes and he shrugged, picking up his saxophone, which shimmered gold beneath the lights.

"Fancy a pint after all this, son?" Dad asked me, casually.

Quite whether there would be an "after all this" remained unclear, but there was no time to think. The drummer began an intricate but catchy beat, followed by deep thrums from the bass section, and finally the brass began to play.

The howls of whatever was listening were smothered by the rising jazz, and it wasn't long before Dad shrugged and started blasting on his sax.

The crowd before me rippled, costumes shifting between the hooded cloaks and the clothes of the jazz musicians they impersonated. Faces extended and altered as bodies shrank and bloated, as if the figures couldn't decide which images they wanted to portray. The band around me were the same. A young Benny Goodman blew his clarinet while a grin spread beyond his cheeks, his fingers flitting between rotten grey and a healthy peach. To Dad's side, Charlie Parker played second sax, looking smooth and chilled except for those moments when his hair morphed into a sagging hood and obscured most of his face.

Someone prodded my back. I turned, and a half-melted version of Billie Holliday gestured towards the microphone, her eyes wider than they should have been, and her teeth as long and thin as cocktail sticks.

The roar of whatever was listening continued to build, now audible over the wild music.

Gods or demons were baying for entertainment.

I was clearly expected to sing; the frontman to a deranged jazz tune I'd never heard.

Before I could start, the nightclub floor burst open.

Like a mouth expelling vomit, a strobing white light erupted into the room. It wasn't just light, though: it had form and substance, and alongside blinding flashes there came nightmarish shadows that stabbed and roiled. There were no curves to be seen within those shapes – just disturbing zigzags, jutting angles, and pentagons that suggested an almost non-Euclidean depth. Obscure dimensions of jet-black and lightning bolts of brilliant white competed in a war of terrible living geometry.

I had seen such shapes before, conjured into being while resting across my father's lap.

Had his designs been visions of these terrible deities? Disturbing configurations called from the void in which these throbbing forms waited, listening for the right moment to arise?

Jazz musicians and cloaked figures fell onto or between the cracks in the unstable ground. Others were slashed apart by jagged darkness or consumed alive by the pulsing, raging white. Through the deafening noise, those musicians whose faces were not hidden by hoods mouthed one unrepentant, gibberish phrase: *BADA-LADA-LO! BADA-LADA-LO!*

Terrified but sensing nothing else to do, I sang. Death was surely imminent, but perhaps something in the music could appease whatever had invaded the club.

The gods of jazz.

The arch-demons of swing.

Into the microphone, I scatted with every "skee-bop" and "doobee-doo" I could muster. It was a struggle to hear the tune beneath the racket of falling masonry and the screeching ululations of the black-and-white monstrosities. I flailed my limbs, striving to remember every Cab Calloway video I'd ever watched and performing my own demented rendition of one of his dances.

Most of the walls caved in and two pillars collapsed with a boom, crushing some of the transforming congregation. Beyond the walls there bubbled and flashed more contrasting shades, seething with savage energy. In spite of the carnage before me – the deaths of cloaked cultists and jazz performers and the things somewhere in between – the white-and-black patterns pulsed to the sound of the music, connected to the jive and the swing and the bop of it all.

Wails of the dying joined the jazz and the diabolical growls. The music seemed to be strengthening these gods or demons, and through the chaos I wondered what they would do when we had finished playing.

Would they break through into the "real world"?

Still "skiddly-bop-ing" and "shawadee-waddee-ing", I swung my head towards the door marked "EXIT".

Sharp-angled tentacles hovered at the portal. They seemed to be thickening, perhaps strengthened by the music.

They would plunge inside once they were strong enough. They would break through.

Whatever happened, I was sure that this would be the last concert I ever attended. If I was right, and the jazz was empowering whatever these colour-contrasted entities were, then I might as well try something to stop it.

So, gathering all the extreme metal ferocity I could scrape up from my soul, I screamed.

"*I am ... theeeeeeeeeeeeeeeeeem!*" I howled, mimicking the climactic cry from one of my favourite black metal songs. I shut my eyes, trying to ignore the terror, the cataclysmic holler of the jazz, and the looming, thrashing demon-gods. Instead, I envisioned myself shrieking to a crowd of grim-faced metal fans, my face painted white with hollowed-out eyes, like a corpse. "*I am ... theeeeeeeeeeeeeeeeeeeeem!*"

I screamed against the music, the cultists, and the jazz-monsters. I railed against the very fact that I had been drawn here. I became the clan of black wizards that the song caused me to envision, chasing invaders from their lands, riding shade-draped steeds and hacking and chopping at those who sought to destroy them.

The flailing of the black-and-white forms decreased. They had no eyes or faces, but I felt sure they were looking at me. They were displeased, but it was not yet enough.

I side-stepped towards the guitarist with the thin moustache – a mutating Django Rheinhardt? – and punched him in the centre of his face. His features imploded, morphing into a cultist's hood before becoming a skull and then a gaping, bloodied pink hole. His arms spread and I wrenched the guitar from him, the strap snapping apart. Awkwardly, holding the weight of the guitar while amateurishly trying to play it, I fingered a barred minor chord and strummed. Unlike Dad, it seemed that this Jazziverse did not instil mystical musical abilities into me, but while the sounds I dragged from the instrument were unpolished and raw, they nonetheless jarred viciously with the music of the jazz players.

"Submission is for the… WEAK!" I screeched into the microphone, quoting another extreme tune. And another: *"Cynical… electric… fucking murderer!"*

The jazz demons seemed to wilt before the sound – or perhaps the monochrome fires were pulling back, weighing me up, and preparing to pounce.

As I continued to howl and assault the guitar, my world became the colour of a dead channel on an old analogue TV set:

black and white and somehow *hungry*. The musicians and the club were gone. All I knew was the guitar, the microphone, and the blizzard of static.

Somewhere beyond it all I could hear the distant tones of the jazz still being performed.

"Dad!" I screamed through the toneless maelstrom. "If you're still playing, *stop!*"

Jagged spikes of white snapped at me like featureless mouths, but while these forms tried to reach me, to destroy me, the clumsy black metal I still played – nothing but thrashed chords without a trace of tremolo – seemed to protect me.

That was, until I was grabbed from behind and yanked backwards, out from the weird fuzz of the static. I wrestled against the other's grasp, catching a glimpse of the eyeless Carl Fontana who held me. Skin bubbled from his chin as his ears and forehead mutated into the grey material of his hood.

I kept shredding at the guitar, but I was running out of energy.

A face appeared at my side, an older version of my own, and my dad shoved Carl Fontana down onto his backside before dragging me back to the mic. The mutant jazz musician's grip around my stomach had driven the breath from my body, so I could no longer exhale – but that was when Dad made a sound I had never heard him produce: a necrotic, throat-searing, black metal scream, so loud I had to cover my ears. It was a cataclysmic, near-genocidal noise, like the war-cry of a thousand conquering barbarians.

That did it.

The black-and-white flames retracted and then exploded, splitting into giant shards of tar-black and magnesium-white that sheared through the musicians and cultists before the stage, smashing away much of what remained of the nightclub.

Dad bellowed into the microphone one more time, veins protruding from his neck and forehead, scowling like the "truest" of black metal vocalists. The jazz-demons retreated and withered, dwindling into thin streaks that sank into the nightclub floor and walls, until every trace of them was gone.

Then everything stopped, and there was only stillness.

Limbs and discarded instruments littered what was left of the ground. Detritus from the stage leaned against the crumbled walls, and scraps of the cultist's cloaks hung from splinters of torn-away masonry. Wherever parts of the nightclub had been wrenched away, there was only black, but not the depthless, vertigo-inducing black of the jazz gods; this was more like the emptiness of space. Most of the ceiling, more than half of the walls, and a great deal of the floor was gone.

The "EXIT" sign and its door had been decimated, too, but where it had stood I could see a narrow line of light, much like the one I'd seen behind Dad's wardrobe before we'd come to the Jazziverse.

"Come on, son," I heard Dad say, under the siren still ringing in my head. "Let's get a pint."

I almost laughed: the bar was still standing. We made our way down the stage stairs and crossed the floor, careful to avoid the gaping black gaps and the silent, broken bodies of several hundred cultists. At the bar, though the bartender was gone, I managed to pour us a decent beer each from the pump.

I looked around at the devastation and the cold, black vacuum beyond it. "Now, Dad. Surely now you'll finally admit that there's power in rock and metal. I mean, those jazz-things were growing until we started screaming and ripping up that guitar."

"Nope," Dad said, and drank his beer. "It was the jazz in me that let me experiment with screaming, and to try something new."

I felt myself scowl. "But that's... you're just..." I floundered. "That's not what happened at all!"

"Bollocks," Dad said, and we drank our drinks and bickered our bickerings until we agreed that it was time to go home.

Jonathan's Afterword

"My dad designed the piece that inspired this story specifically for this anthology, and it was as much his title that gave me the plotline as the image itself. He called it 'Ultra Jazz Demons'. When I look at this design, I find it terribly unsettling. Many of dad's designs are symmetrical, or as near as they can be, but this is chaos. While I could have picked out its intricacies and interpreted different sections of the design to inspire different aspects of the tale, I preferred to embrace the overwhelming atmosphere of violence and disorder that it radiated. I imagined a surreal, hungry entity, drunk on its own desires, and urging those who stood before it to... what? That was the question I sought to answer, in a tale that (somewhat self-indulgently) features both myself and my father."

THIRD EYE

LYDIAN FAUST

Piney was surprised at how easy it was to pry out Jenna's Third-Eye. With a few clicks, the Eye released itself from the girl's fresh corpse and batted its silver lashes at Piney. Was it *flirting* with her? She laughed hysterically. The whole thing was too bizarre. An Eye flirting with the girl who murdered its owner. Piney laid the Third-Eye on the nightstand beside the body of its former host; its smothered host. Jenna hadn't even struggled. Extremely bizarre. Not that Piney was a seasoned killer, but she'd seen shows. It was if Jenna didn't mind the pillow pressed upon her pretty face. Gracious 'til the bitter end.

A pageant queen with a seemingly perfect life, Jenna could've been the type of high-school princess everyone loved to hate, but they all just loved her. She was sunny, smart, and kind, and never boastful about her minor celebrity status. Though she didn't have friends over to her house, Jenna was always out and about town, surrounded by her devoted flock. Jocks loved her. Burn-outs loved her. Even the nerds loved her. Piney probably should've loved her, too. When the other kids called her "poor Pocahontas McGhee," Jenna didn't stick up for Piney exactly, but she'd never joined in on the bullying. She'd just frown and give Piney a pained look. Always the same expression of pity. Piney didn't want the girl's pity. Didn't want or need anyone's damn pity. She'd felt sorry enough for herself her whole life. Druggy parents dead. Heroin overdose. Raised by Gran in the old family home, the last of the old houses left standing as urban sprawl consumed the others, making way for new suburbs. With new suburbs came new students, none of whom looked like Piney or her grandmother, whose ancestors had been there for ages.

Gran was proud, and she tried to instil that pride in Piney.

"Our people have been here the longest," she'd say, "and we worked hard to help build this town. We've always worked hard, same as anyone. Don't need anyone looking their noses down at us, Pine, and we certainly don't need their charity."

Piney wished her Gran would budge just once on her refusal of charity. Piney knew there wasn't going to be a Third-Eye there for her that summer on Unboxing Day. Her portal would remain closed. They just didn't have enough money. They lived on the fixed income of her late grandfather's pension and what was left of the life insurance. There was a special grant for "Indigenous Peoples" awarding enough for an off-brand Third-Eye, but Gran flatly refused. So, that week before sophomore year, while all of her classmates were unboxing their Third-Eyes (MindzEye and iEye being the biggest status brands), Piney was throwing a pity-party of one. Her misfortune consumed her. Abandoned by her fucking dragon-chasing parents. She hoped there was a Hell and they were frying. Her earliest friends had moved away. She was now a stranger in her own land. Even her online friends had abandoned the old social media stomping grounds now that they all had their Eyes. Left her in the digital dust. The kids at school didn't pick on her much anymore, at least. They mostly just ignored her. She wasn't sure which was worse. Forever alone, through no fault of her own. All of her rage, all of her bitterness, all of the injustices heaped upon her comingled and concentrated into a laser-beam-focused obsession with the Third-Eye. Without the Third-Eye, she'd always be an outsider looking in. It was eating her up. She was going to get one, no matter the cost.

Piney pulled the pillow from Jenna's faced and looked into the girl's lifeless blue eyes. It was unreal how beautiful she was, even now. A porcelain doll. So fucking perfect. So unfair. Piney smacked the corpse hard across the cheek, then pummelled the girl's chest with her bony fists, harder, faster, releasing the pain, splitting her own thin skin. Furious tears fell to salt the wound. A weblike stroke on her cheek snapped her out of the tirade. Piney's eyes widened to see the Third-Eye standing up on seven fine needlepoint legs, the eighth gently caressing her face.

"Are you alive?" she whispered.

The Eye blinked rapidly in response. Moving its appendage from her cheek to the closed portal of spiral teeth above her eyebrows, it moved her hair aside and gave the portal a series of taps. The aperture opened, the maw hungry for the Eye. Piney was elated, yet nervous. Surely it couldn't be that easy?

Today was the first time that everything seemed to just fall into place for her. In second-hour, American History, Ms. Richmond assigned Piney and Jenna as project partners. Piney had put her head down when Ms. Richmond cheerfully announced that their new Third-Eyes would make research for the project much easier.

The teacher flushed when she saw Piney, realizing that the girl must be the only sophomore without a Third-Eye. That would explain the child's awful bangs. Piney had cut them that morning with kitchen scissors, while Gran was still asleep. The ragged fringe was an attempt at camouflaging her lack of Eye, but it had just made it all the more obvious. Not that the other students didn't already know she wasn't connected to them.

Ms. Richmond noticed that Jenna was the only one looking upon Piney with pity instead of smirking at her, so decided to pair them. It was that final look of pity that sealed her fate. Pairing the girls was a temporary solution but Ms. Richmond knew that unless Piney's grandmother could be convinced to take the grant, the girl would have to be transferred to a special needs classroom. The girls pushed their desks together to discuss project plans, and Jenna enthusiastically suggested that she come over to Piney's place after school to work on it. Piney readily agreed. It was the perfect opportunity; being Friday, her grandmother would be down at the bingo hall until dinnertime.

"This is your house? It's so big!" Jenna exclaimed, clearly taken aback by the ivy-choked Victorian. Despite peeling paint and missing shingles, the old place still had an aura of grandeur.

"Yeah, that surprises you?" Piney said dryly.

"Oh, no, sorry, I just thought..."

"Don't worry about it."

Piney knew what she thought. Knew what everyone thought: that she lived in a trailer or some sort of fucking teepee.

"Gran's not home, so we have the place to ourselves. Did you need to text, or beam, or whatever the hell it is you can do now, to your parents and let them know you're over here?"

"Oh, they don't care. I'm never home before seven."

"Cool."

"My room's on the third floor. You wanna soda?"

"I don't drink soda, but water would be great, thanks."

Of course, a beauty queen doesn't drink soda.

They settled on Piney's bed, with Piney's laptop and some notebooks, which Jenna regarded bemusedly. Piney heard a soft whirring noise followed by Jenna's giggle.

"What's so funny?" Piney snapped.

"Sorry! It was just something one of my friends sent me just now," she tapped her Third-Eye. "Sorry, I'll turn it off."

Piney scowled. They were probably making fun of her in there, in that world she was locked out of.

"Hey, Piney, I like your new bangs, by the way. Very... interesting look."

That was what did it. A switch flipped and Piney took the girl down, grabbing the pillow and pushing it down over her face. Jenna gave a single muffled cry, which sounded more like a laugh, unsettling Piney, who pressed harder. Jenna didn't fight. Piney braced herself for kicks and scratches, but the girl just went slack. She kept the pillow pressed for a good fifteen minutes until her arms began to tingle. Probably overkill, but she wasn't an expert.

Now Piney had what she deserved. Now it was time for her to truly see.

"C'mon then. I'm ready."

The Eye crawled in and firmly attached itself inside her portal. At once, all of the windows opened in her brain. Infinite data streams, a cacophony of chatter, songs, an overstimulation of discordant harmonies, flashes of other realms, a bombardment of sex and slaughter, advertisements, evangelists shouting at the damned, popularity contests, friend versus friend, tunnels sucking her down to back-channel pits where--

"Stop! Close!" Piney screamed.

The windows slammed shut. Her head throbbed, knives in the temples. No one told her it would be like this. They said it would be pleasant. Seamless. Intuitive. Something had to be very wrong. Stumbling down the hall to the bathroom, she grabbed a headband to push her bangs back and peered into the mirror. The Third-Eye was closed, silver lashes cast down.

Open, she thought.

The lashes fluttered up and Piney found herself looking simultaneously at the Eye in the mirror with her human eyes and out from the Third-Eye itself. A video-player icon, like an old movie-theatre projector, popped up in her field of vision. Ah, maybe these were instructions, perhaps some sort of Third-Eye beginner's manual. The Eye probably just needed to be reset.

Play.

The reel began to spin, and her image in the looking glass was replaced by that of an unfamiliar room. She was looking down the length of a long dining table, set for three. Piney glanced down at a stranger's hand, French manicured, holding a silver fork. At the far end of the table sat a middle-aged man and woman, professionally dressed. They were scowling.

"Jenna, darling, do you really have to scrape your fork like that?"

Piney stiffened. Jenna? She was seeing, what, the girl's memories? A recording?

The fork dropped, clanking the edge of the plate.

"I don't care for it," she heard Jenna's voice say softly.

"Jenna, sweetie, please--"

"Don't coddle her, damn it!" The man Piney assumed was Jenna's dad slammed his fist on the table hard enough to topple

Jenna's crystal water goblet. It shattered, sending shards onto her plate. The Eye roved down to show the glass pieces poking up from a purplish-black mass, quivering on the Dalton china.

"See what you made me do?" the father yelled.

"I won't be able to get more until next week," sighed the mother, shaking her coiffed head.

"Not hungry, don't need it," Jenna mumbled, picking a shard from the quivering mass.

"Ow! Shit!"

As the glass sliced the length of her thumb, a viscous green fluid seeped from the cut, drops of it sizzling through the china below. Jenna hissed, and when she brought her thumb to her mouth, Piney saw what looked like scales jutting from the edges of the wound. Piney felt bile rise.

What the fuck was she seeing?

She told herself that this must've been some sort of film project Jenna made. Maybe an audition tape or something. She knew the girl had been in a few local commercials. That had to be what it was. Whatever it was, Piney had seen enough.

"Stop!" Piney commanded.

The Third-Eye did not stop.

The mother crossed her arms. A film slid over her eyes, leaving only slitted pupils.

"Jenna! You know you have a photo-shoot in the morning!"

"Mom, chill! It'll heal by then!"

"Don't you dare tell your mother to 'chill,' young lady! And we don't waste food in this house! Now go see your sister! Ten lashes this time! I'd better be able to count the marks."

Sister?

"Yes, dad," Jenna replied mechanically, taking the keycard from his outstretched hand.

Jenna made her way down the hall, stopping by the bathroom to bandage her scaly thumb (which had already stopped oozing). She opened a linen-closet and selected a whip, hanging among a dozen others. Then, further into the closet she pressed down on a shelf of tea towels and the wall swung inwards to reveal a set of winding stairs. At the bottom stood an iron door without a knob. Jenna flashed the keycard at the small panel beside the door and it slid sideways to reveal a small chamber. The Eye zoomed in on the misshapen thing hunkering in the dimly-lit corner before Jenna's voice commanded the Eye to close. Piney's view reverted back to her own image in the mirror, but she could still hear Jenna's voice. The Eye hadn't stopped recording the audio.

"I'm sorry, little sister. He said ten lashes this time."

Piney heard an inhuman cry, akin to a braying donkey.

"I'll make it quick. Sorry. I hate to do this. But you know I can't have any marks. I wish things didn't have to be this way. I wish you could be like us, come upstairs. But you know it doesn't hurt you as much as it does me."

Piney heard the whip crack against something hard, then came the horrific cries, the braying, over and over.

"Stop! Stop!" Piney shouted, scratching at the Eye.

The Eye would not stop.

The Eye wanted her to hear, needed her to *see*.

Piney frantically searched the bathroom for something to dig it out.

"Pine! I'm home! Pine? You up there? Come down here, I got somethin' for ya!"

The audio stopped, closing at the sound of her grandmother's voice.

Gran.

Piney sighed in relief.

Wait, no! Shit! Gran! Jenna's body!

How long had it been? Fuck, what was she thinking? She hadn't thought this through at all.

Think, Pine, think!

Pulling the headband off, Piney pushed her bangs over her forehead and threw on her baseball hat hanging from the towel hook. She ran back to her bedroom and locked the door, unable to bring herself to look at the corpse. She'd have to deal with disposal later. There was very little chance of Gran discovering Jenna up here, anyway. Her grandmother's arthritic hips kept her mostly to the first-floor these days. Piney rushed down the flights of stairs to the kitchen.

"Hey Gran, how was bingo? Oooh, is that fried chicken?"

Act natural.

Piney reached for the bucket, but her grandmother playfully slapped her away.

"The Colonel's finest! But first, Pine, my girl, I have a surprise for you!"

"A surprise for me?"

"I won bingo tonight, Pine! Quadruple pot! Can you believe it? After all these years? Oh, that Francine was so jealous, ha! You should've seen her face! Anyway, I stopped by after and got you something very special! Now you just sit right there at the table and lemme get it out."

Piney wiped her clammy hands on her jeans while Gran rummaged through her purse. She turned back around triumphantly, holding up a palm-sized box.

A MindzEye box.

"Only the best Third-Eye for my Piney!"

"Oh, Gran, you really shouldn't have..."

"Hush now! Listen, I know you were sore at me for not takin' that grant, Pine, but you know my stance on hand-outs. I was scrimping and sellin' a few old things here and there to get you one eventually anyway, but luck just happened to strike tonight!"

What had she done?

"Oh, Gran, I..."

"Shh! C'mon, let's get you up-to-date with your friends!"

Before she could protest, Gran came over and whipped off Piney's baseball cap. The girl shrank back as she frowned down at her.

"Girl, what've you done to your hair?"

"I, um, cut some bangs."

"Bangs? Are those back in style? You know I can't keep up with you kids. I'm sorry to tell you dear, but they look awful! Don't worry, they'll grow. Anyhow, enough about that, I don't mean to make you feel bad. Here now, let's put this sucker in!"

Gran swept the fringe back from her forehead and Piney felt the click of the Third-Eye opening, blinking at her grandmother.

"Pine! Piney, what have you done? How?"

The shock caused the old woman to stumble backward, upsetting a chair that took her down with it, her grey head hitting the sharp edge of the island counter before slamming the tiles below. Blood pooled the checkered floor beneath Gran's skull and the Eye zoomed-in for a detailed shot. Gran's gaze was empty. No breath. No pulse. Piney knew she couldn't call for help. They'd find Jenna.

Shit! Jenna!

"Quite the predicament you're in," she heard Jenna say.

"Close!" Piney commanded.

The Eye closed and shed a silver tear.

"I'm still here," Jenna laughed in her ear.

Piney jerked back to see the girl, the girl she killed, standing in her kitchen.

"This isn't real! This is just the Eye! Close! You're dead, Jenna! Dead!"

"Oh, yeah, it never lasts long," Jenna said nonchalantly, poking through the bucket of fried chicken before selecting a drumstick and taking a bite.

"Mmm, so good," she mumbled, "you know my mom never lets me eat this stuff."

A film clouded her eyes as she sucked the juices from her fingertips.

"WHAT THE FUCK ARE YOU?" Piney screamed.

"I," Jenna said brightly, advancing towards the trembling girl, "am your new sister. My younger sister had a terrible accident. Sadly, she's passed. I've been a wreck without her, but it doesn't do any good to dwell on these things. I know you must be horribly upset right now. So sad. Don't worry about your grandmother and all of this," Jenna waved her hand dismissively, "this mess. I feel so sorry for you, Piney. Always have. Such a pity. None of this is your fault. I forgive you. I know how it feels to be different from everyone else, I truly do. Things are going to change. You don't have to go back to school. We're sisters now. We have a special room at the house, ready just for you."

She smiled sweetly and held her hand out to help Piney up.

That was Jenna, gracious til the end.

Lydian's Afterword

"Looking at my op art inspiration, I immediately thought of it as an eye. It was mesmerizing. A radiating iris. As I often do when writing, I put on my music video playlist. A video from Tool, one of my favourite bands, popped up. The song was "Third Eye," and the refrain, "prying open my third eye, prying open my third eye," is what inspired the violent first line of my story and set the desperate and unsettling tone for the rest of the tale. Set vaguely in the near-future, in a society of technological haves and have-nots, I wanted to explore the consequences of one of these "have-nots" prying open a Third-Eye."

Brother, Can You Spare A Paradigm?

DAVID COURT

There are eleven people in this bar, and three of them are me.

Hell of an ice-breaker, ain't it? If I ever get around to writing my memoirs, it'll all be fully explained there. For now, just take it that a messy encounter with the fabled Albarossa Crystal in an old case ended up creating several duplicates of yours truly. Blackstone Senior had asked me to put them out of their misery, but it reeked a little too much of suicide for me. As it was, I called in a few favours and got their memories "altered" and still, to this day, our paths sometimes cross. A bit of the old Blackstone magic and they don't recognize each other, or more importantly, *me*.

All three of us regularly gravitate here for the same reason, but only I know what that reason *is*.

The *Toot Suite* is one of a handful of jazz bars in Manhattan, and you'd be hard pressed to tell one from the other. They're all dark basements with inadequate lighting and overpriced liquor, filled with cigarette smoke so thick you half expect the hound of the Baskervilles to emerge. There's a difference here though, and she's on stage right now.

Before you look at her, just listen. That's a helluva voice, ain't it? I used to think Scat was nonsense, just a bunch of messed-up syllables and wordless vocables – that was, until her.

Cassandra Solomon.

Listen. Properly listen, I mean. Breathe it in, like you would a cigarette. You go in any other jazz club and you'd have to strain to hear over the chatter and clinking of glasses. There's an appropriate reverence here, and everybody stays shut up for her. She's the Queen, and we're nothing more than her oh-so-loyal subjects.

You can make out words, if you listen hard enough. *Feel* them, pressing against your heart. That's *poetry*, man - poetry from a soul deeper than the Atlantic. That's a voice that's properly lived – from somebody who's had their heart lifted up into the sun as many times as it's been shattered like ice.

Now look.

Admittedly, she's a sight to behold. That shimmering blue dress that moves like the night, that long black hair, that pearlescent white skin pierced by bright red lipstick, those gams that just don't know *when* to stop – but that ain't the first thing you notice, is it?

Be honest, you expected somebody older, didn't you? She's young, but with an old soul. She's the kind of person to make you believe reincarnation is the real deal, that anybody with a voice like that must have lived a dozen lifetimes.

Her bass player has chops at the best of times, but tonight he's smokin' more than the salmon that hangs glassy-eyed in the fishmongers next door. They're riffing off each other as the song builds to its close, the tempo raised up a notch and the crowd captivated by every moment, nodding their heads, tapping their feet, or both.

The musicians fall silent as Cassandra holds on to that one last note like a drowning woman clinging on for life. You can feel it against your skin, hugging your bones.

As she stops singing, the room remains deathly quiet for a single beat. Then, there's applause so noisy and enthusiastic, you'll swear the room was filled with four times as many people.

She steps gracefully from the stage, and is handed a bunch of flowers by an eager fan. She acknowledges him with a wink and a smile, and purposefully strides towards me. I read the situation; the look in her eyes, the speed of her steps, the suddenly-serious expression on her face.

She'll lean in and ask me to meet her backstage. "Alone", she'll insist, her voice tinged with worry and concern. She'll step past me, her fingertips brushing against my shoulder for a moment longer than is comfortable for either of us, and she'll quickly vanish. Her perfume will linger in the air long after she's gone.

My predictions are, as to be expected, accurate. Unless I'm very much mistaken – and I'm not - her perfume's *Joy* by Jean Patou.

#

I know full well that she'll wait for me, so I savour the rest of my Bullshot while the next band sets up. The beefiness of the broth threatens to – but doesn't quite – overwhelm the heat from the vodka, cayenne, and Tabasco, and it goes down easier than a five-dollar whore. They've just started playing as I approach the ape guarding the backstage area. I know he's already been warned of my arrival, and he steps aside to let me in without so much as a grunted "good evening".

Right, this is as good a moment as we'll get, so there are two things we need to get clear at this stage.

I know you're there and listening to me. Blackstone Senior let me in on this whole cosmic charade thing and that we're being watched from forces unseen, so I'm just being polite in explaining the situation to you as best I can.

Secondly, within a short while, you'll be wondering why I seem to know so much about what is going to happen before it actually happens. It may make me come across as a little smug or over-confident, but that's not the case.

I'm what Blackstone nicknamed a *Vorticist*.

A clever little part of my subconscious sees the patterns in things – the patterns in *everything*. You might think everything you do is down to your own free will, but it turns out the universe is just one big machine – you're a tiny little clockwork cog in this vast contraption, and everything you've done or will do has all been carefully planned out in advance.

"That's bull," you're thinking. "I'll just do something unpredictable."

I've seen it all. Turns out, you were *always* going to react that way.

Mind-fuck, ain't it?

So, I'm gifted – or *cursed*, you might argue – with being able to see these patterns. Sometimes minutes' worth, sometimes hours. It sounds great, but it fucks with you on a daily basis.

Imagine sitting down at the theatre, or for a movie or piece of music, and you already know exactly what you're in for. You already know how every bite of that Porterhouse steak or that expensive wine is gonna taste.

That's why I always end up here in the *Toot Suite* Jazz club, and probably why my doppelgangers do too. Blackstone informs me that the gift didn't pass over to them when they were unexpectedly created, but instinct keeps guiding them back.

Turns out my "talent" has a blind spot when it comes to improvised jazz.

I can't read or predict it. Every chord progression is a revelation, every modal harmony and plucked or hammered note a unique pleasure. I can lose myself in the musical journey, temporarily freed from the burden of this precognition. And the discordant chaos when the musicians "free blow" and ignore the chord changes, improvising as they see fit, it's nothing short of bliss. And improvised Jazz doesn't come any better than at the *Toot Suite.*

I knock on the door, already knowing it'll be opened just after the second knock. It's the club owner, a sour kraut named Max who made a tidy profit from WWII and built his name in the village as a property owner. Both the man and his temper are notoriously short, and I remember him breaking the fingers of a musician who cheekily addressed him as "Jazz Hans". Poor schmuck couldn't play his instrument for two months. Max argued he could barely play it before.

Max looks me up and down – mostly up, due to his diminished stature – before leaving the room and leaving us alone. Cassandra has her back to me, but stares at my reflection in the mirror. I'm looking forward to the way she's about to say my name, the words seductively lingering on her lips as though she's trying to seduce me. The hint of a Southern accent she's been tryin' to disguise that occasionally slips through.

"Rick Bannerette."

She turns to face me, extending a slender hand. My acumen reveals to me that the kiss I'd intended to plant on the back of her porcelain white hand gets me nothing but a vicious glare, so I change tack and gently shake it instead.

"The name I got stencilled on my door is backwards, but I think that's what it says. What can I do for the Manhattan Queen of Jazz?"

"Josef tells me you've got a penchant for dealing for unusual cases, Mr. Bannerette."

Josef works the bar here; a giant of a man and a relative of Max. I got him out of a fix a couple of months back when the ghost of a dead Josef from a sideways reality decided to start hauntin' him through mirrors.

"It's been known. Let's get a drink and you can tell me all about it. I'm guessing a lady like yourself is fond of…"

She'll smile and… what? I'm suddenly overwhelmed by a flood of images, a surge of shattered fractals. They're hanging in the air like shards of broken mirror, each with a different suspended image of Cassandra within. She's in a variety of different dressing rooms, in an assortment of different outfits. I hear a chorus of her voice requesting a hundred different drinks; *champagne, white wine spritzer, bourbon, single malt, red wine.* This is different from the blissful void I get when listening to the jazz – here I'm seeing *every* possibility, *all* eventualities.

A myriad of assorted Cassandras dash to help me, some supporting me, some too late to stop my fall. Just as I think I can't cope with the torrent of sights and sounds assaulting my senses, everything settles again into just a single, solitary paradigm.

Her arms are around me, and Jean Patou's *Joy* rouses me like smelling salts. I blink and try and regain some sense of dignity, blinded though I am to what lies ahead. It's all I can do to concentrate on the here and now, let alone beyond that.

"Are you okay, Rick?"

"I am. Just a little dizzy, is all."

Within moments, I'm seated and there's a glass of water in my hand. I typically only drink water when it's in the form of frozen cubes floating in a glass of rye, but today I'll make an exception. I've been feeling run down recently, and I'm hoping this empty feeling will pass. Time to at least try to get back into character.

"Thank you. So, what's your problem?"

She rummaged around in her handbag, pulling out an assortment of varied makeups and packs of Juicy Fruit.

"I don't know how scared I should be, Mr Bannerette. Everywhere I go, I keep finding these. Somebody keeps sending them through my mailbox, leaving them in my dressing room. I throw them in the trash, new ones appear."

Suddenly, her eyes lit up with recognition, and she pulled a card from the dim recesses of her seemingly infinite bag. It was the size of a playing card with a dull, matte black back. I held out my hand for it, only now noticing my trembling fingers.

Even with my precognition on the fritz, I felt a sense of dread. Perhaps it was just a lifetime's worth of instinct, but I was loath to turn the card over and look at the face.

At first, I thought it a spiral, but with a closer look, it was a pattern of concentric circles. A pattern of jagged black and grey teeth, a trick of the eye giving it the illusion of movement. There was a solid black sphere set at the centre, like the staring pupil of a monstrous eye set against that two-tone iris.

I recognise it instantly. I've spent so much of my life literally ahead of myself, that I sometimes to forget to look *back*. The card falls from my fingers, gently fluttering on the floor, and my heart sinks with it.

It's a *trap*. I was cursed the moment I laid eyes on that damned thing, and, thanks to my power, my mind's eye saw it. It's a trap I'd fallen into before it was even sprung, and before I could do anything to protect myself from its power.

Same as how you'd get if you stared at a bright light for too long, the negative afterimage on the card is imprinted on my retina. In all honesty, I'd never intended for this to be an origin story, but certain elements have now become critical. I was little more than a kid at the time – off with Blackstone on one of his crazy adventures. "The Case of the Pilfered Participle", it came to be known as in his journals. Presumably that rolled off the pen easier than "The Case Where Your Kid Sidekick Ends up Staring into The Heart of Infinity and Getting Crazy Precognitive Powers".

I remember it as though it were yesterday. It was the day when Blackstone learned the hard way that if you insist a kid doesn't do something, he's going to go and do it. I heard he had a kid of his own after our escapades – followed him into the magic game.

You're familiar with the Nietzsche quote, something like "If you stare into the abyss, the abyss stares back at you"? I'd always assumed that the abyss was a metaphor – turned out that it was an *actual* abyss, somewhere deep in Chang Tang in Tibet. The ancient grimoires called it *God's Eye*, but the locals had another term for it - *God's Sphincter*. Anyways, despite the advice of my highly trained and educated mentor, I stared right down there – and something stared back at me; a brilliant white eye, glaring at me from the heart of the multiverse.

And in that pattern, I saw the inverse of the pattern on the card, which ended up imprinting on my soul and turning me – in Blackstone's words – into a Vorticist.

They've led me right here, like a rookie. They've taken advantage of my three weaknesses – jazz, bars, and pretty ladies – to rid me of my powers and leave me exposed and vulnerable. After years of trying, they've finally mastered the replication of the pattern of the anti-abyss and switched off my gift.

"Get out of here!" I scream at Cassandra. She doesn't need telling twice, as scared of my sudden outburst as anything else I might be warning her about. I hear him before I see him, the grinding of machinery and the pounding of pistons accompanying his arrival.

If you ever go anywhere real remote, miles away from people and their incessant chattering and motor cars, just *listen*. If you're lucky, and the wind is right, you might hear them. The gentle whoosh of pressurised air or steam coming from pneumatic machinery, the tick-tocking of cogs pushing cogs pushing cogs. These are the sounds of the quantum machineries that power reality, the perpetual motion machines that will never stop as they operate to infinitesimal precision, driving the universe and everything in it.

When he arrived, that fragile membrane that separated us from those infernal machines is peeled back slightly. I know who I'm dealing with now – there's only one foe I know who knows of the source of my powers, the only one who would have even stood a fighting chance of capturing the exact precision needed for the anti-abyss to nullify them.

There's that oh-so-familiar sense of synaesthesia that I'm used to from our previous encounters, as I'm gagging from the acrid scent of him screaming my name in defiance. He unfolds in front of me like an idea given detail, suddenly standing there as a series of small black and white geometric cubes approximating a human form.

The Futurist.

We'd met before, but I'd always had the upper hand. Despite his aggressive and unpredictable nature, his "smear of violence" as he called it, I could read him like a book. An abstract pop-up book, admittedly, but a book nonetheless. He couldn't defeat an opponent who could predict his every move, and I'd been a constant thorn in his minimalist side.

Hence the trap.

"How does it feel?" he bellows. His voice was always disconcerting, accompanied, as it was, by an invisible atonal choir. "How does it feel to be stuck in the here and now?"

He doesn't even give me chance to answer. Reality ripples around him like an ill-fitting swimsuit, and we were suddenly both elsewhen and elsewhere. This was his realm; a vast, monochrome, grid-scored landscape. In all honesty, I was relieved he'd moved our conflict to a different plane – anything to remove the risk of innocent bystanders being caught up, transformed into Dadaist concepts – or worse.

I throw a punch, but he's altered the laws of physics before it gets anywhere near him. Any momentum my fist had is lost, and my knuckles simply brush against him. His own retaliation is swift and brutal – I'm suddenly standing about three feet away, two pints of blood down. He's kept that where I was, and I briefly see it suspended there in a rough humanoid shape, before it splashes across the flat ground.

The battle has hardly begun and – thanks to the blood-loss – I can feel myself growing faint. For his next trick, he undoes the tonsillectomy I had a year or so back; the infected tissue is suddenly there at the back of my gullet, inflated and sore. I can barely breathe, clutching at my throat. Any protective wards I had that would have served me, I'm now incapable of reciting.

The synaesthesia is back, and I can feel the barbed touch of his gloating laughter against my fingertips.

Think, Rick, think.

A zen-like moment of tranquillity passes over me as the answer becomes clear. Trying to ignore his triumphant bellowing, I close my eyes tight and concentrate. The negative image on the card is still there, a faint afterimage burned across the surface of my retina. And a negative of a negative is…

The image from the abyss is there, faint, but humming with potential power. Before the afterimage fades and is gone for good, I call on the last of its reserves.

I can see the Futurist's next attack, signposted in front of me as clearly as if I were watching it unfold on a cinema screen – the potential killing blow. A skilled feint sees him miss me, several important nerve points exposed and vulnerable. With the few moments I have to spare, a self-taught move from an amalgam of several schools of martial artistry sees the Futurist at my mercy.

It's not one to kill, but it *is* one that hurts. He's still screaming as reality deposits us back in the dressing room, everything temporarily paralysed by my attack except for his mouth, tongue, and vocal chords. I chose that specific attack for a very specific reason.

He's a considerably less imposing foe, stripped of his reality-altering powers. Less imposing still after I retrieve Dorothy – my trusty Smith & Wesson 29 - from my jacket pocket and plug his head with a cylinder full of .44 Magnum rounds.

I don't need any powers of precognition to know what his head will look like after that.

Josef and Max are at the door, stopping Cassandra in her tracks so she doesn't have to see what's left of my arch-nemesis. My throat is healed, the tonsillectomy restored.

"You won't be getting no more of those calling cards," I reassure her on the way past. She doesn't look particularly comforted.

"What do we tell the police, Mr. Bannerette?" asks Josef, dumbfounded. "What if they need to speak to you?"

"Tell them I'm on the next flight to Tibet, Josef," I smiled.

David's Afterword

"The first thing I picked up from the design was, at a gut level, the impression of a staring eye. And I expanded upon that, deciding the story would feature a private eye - which seemed to work well with a jazz theme as well. And what would happen if you stared back into that giant eye?

"It incorporates the old chestnut of a dick and a dame, but hopefully turns that on its head a little bit. Hope you enjoy. It's been a real delight moving away from horror and into simply weird fiction again."

THE CRUELLEST GIFT

J. G. CLAY

The eyes did not look right.

Hue, shade, emotion; not one of these pieces fitted into the jigsaw provided by nightmare. The creature stalking Kayvan's fever dreams was a study in dominance, power and cruelty. What lay before him on canvas possessed stature and bearing but its gaze was beneficent, doe-eyed, meek. It reminded him too much of the carpenter-turned messiah who adorned every hallway of his childhood schools. That was not good enough.

This creature was no messiah. Its arms were splayed, the gesture an invitation to fight not to welcome lost souls to the flock. Large white teeth bared in a sneer of defiance, head thrust forward. This being oozed power, confidence and malice. Or it would do.

If the eyes were right.

Kayvan stepped back, scanning the monster's ebony visage, transposing the living sweating thing of dream onto his own interpretation.

"You're more dangerous than that," he muttered vacantly. "So much more."

Fragments of hallucination ambushed him; booming joyful laughter fetched to his ears on a foul sea breeze, droplets of oily ocean water coating his skin, his own despair mingling with that of the bleeding faceless man propping this monster's leg up with a flayed oozing back.

The creature favoured Kayvan with a secretive smile, raising its heavy brow. Wide arms, coiled with ropes of muscle dropped down to its sides, condensation dripping from its fingertip.

"Luck is a widow, awaiting the moment when her wounded heart can open once again or be doomed to solitude ever more." Kayvan, open-mouthed, searched for a reply. Pointing a long-taloned finger downward at the crouched man beneath its right foot, it continued. "This one here? The widow passed by. She abandoned him. Poor mite. Once Lady Luck deserts you, there is only me. House Abbaddon awaits this one." It flexed its leg, bearing down on the kneeling unfortunate. Bone cracked, an arm splaying outward and into an unnatural angle as the man was pummelled into the ground. Tortured screaming filled the air.

It had been his own. Thrust from sleep by his own howling, Kayvan sat up, sweat-drenched, the sound of crunching bone and tearing ligament echoing through his mind. He had leapt from his bed, sleep forgotten as the compulsion to document his dream seized him. Three days on and the work was nearly done.

If he could get the eyes right.

Dropping the brush, he flexed his aching hand. His fingers ached, his right ankle swollen, his breath sticky and rancid as it sloughed over his tongue. It was time for a break. All work and no play made Kayvan… dull? He laughed sadly. Life was not dull. Far from it. The shame of it was that he had not sought the attention he now had.

Yes, he nodded. A beer on the balcony would refresh and revive.

Wiggling his stiff fingers, he smiled at the beast.

"Be right back. Y'all be good now," he drawled, in a passable Deep South accent. The creature seemed to nod and wink in reply. Unsure of what he had seen, Kayvan froze.

Real or a fatigue-induced delusion? Either explanation made sense. His natural reserves were taxed to the hilt, a legacy of his drive and obsession. Unusual occurrences were a feature of his life. The creature did not move again.

He turned away from the monster, the black beach and the luckless card-holder. The world of *The Handsworth Limbostan* awaited beyond the rattling loose windows of his flat. There was so much to be seen and Kayvan was a keen observer.

"A gift can be cruel."

The prisoner looked ahead, studying the bare white walls as they rolled by. There was no need for reply. There never was. Every journey to the Killing Floor was identical; the smooth roll of the wheelchair, the chafing of the restraints, the bite of memory sparked by that one phrase. A voice, thick with inflection, rang in his ears.

I don't give presents normally. Have this one on me.

Lucent's flesh prickled, the livid scar on his cheek contracting as he remembered the bite of the blade, the sizzle as skin parted and nerve shrank before steel. He dug his fingernails into his palms, embracing present day pain to shield against past agony. Phillipe droned on. Not even the Gods could stop him when the need for a lecture arose. Lucent disconnected. He knew Phillipe's routine by wrote.

"A gift can also be kind, you know."

Another memory surfaced like ocean flotsam, bobbing as it awaited retrieval. He saw a box, wrapped in gaudy paper. His young heart quickened in anticipation. Lucent squeezed tighter, reburying the recollection with little ceremony or thought. Phillipe fell silent, the hum of rubber wheels on black concrete tracking their collective journey. Satisfied that he had regained control, Lucent opened his eyes. The walls in this sector were adorned with pentagonal shapes, scattered haphazardly around. There was no rhyme or reason to their layout, no sense, mathematically or aesthetically. Some were painted up high and close to the ceiling, others low down, thick black outlines merging with the obsidian floor. He never wondered about their significance. Interior décor held no interest unless it was the raw crimson of an opened chest or the beige mucus-slicked coils of guts spilling from torn muscle. The internal layout of the human body, especially one still twitching and bleeding, held true beauty in his eye. Nothing else could compare.

Phillipe cleared his throat, struck by a thought he wished to share with his captive audience. Lucent wasn't going anywhere. Straps held him firmly down in the antique wheelchair; a necessary step, he had been told. The last escape attempt made an impression on Phillipe and his confederates.

Lucent was too valuable to lose.

"What we do here is a gift, both cruel and kind, don't you think?"

Again, the prisoner offered no reply.

"Separating the non-cooperative is a cruel step, I know. Believe me, I have no taste for the slaughter we allow you to indulge in. But, it's the only way to keep the peace for the majority."

A sigh flavoured the air with garlic and something mysterious yet familiar. Rolling his eyes, Lucent worried his bottom lip. Phillipe irritated him. Every facet of his being scraped Lucent's nerves raw. He had the look of a toad; protruding eyes, a downward-turned mouth, sheeny unhealthy skin, hair clotted with product and scraped back to showcase a pockmarked forehead. His frame was ungainly, unproportioned, long arms and legs glued to a short pot-bellied torso. His taste in designer suits only added to the shambolic aura he cast. The clothes were impeccable but not made for such an ungainly creature.

Phillipe papered over his physical shortcomings with a sadism Lucent was all too familiar with. The angry knotted curve running from his left temple down to his mouth was testament enough. It was 'a gift', presented to him as payment for laughing at Phillipe's tie. He never laughed again.

The corridor curved gently to the left as they drew closer to the Killing Room. Lucent relaxed a little, relieved. He would finally be free of the wheelchair, Phillipe and his comfortable cell. Two months without a Kill Job left him nervy and unfulfilled. Even the snuff porn they allowed him had not quelled his restlessness. The urge to kill was strong. Not strong enough to break through his captor's security, however. Something within this white-washed prison dampened his gift.

In his first few months, Lucent had tried every trick in his formidable arsenal; astral projection, telekinetic mutilation, mentally-induced spontaneous combustion. Failures, all of them. Deep in his trance, his visions of death were wiped clean by a white hell, eternal blankness. Then came entrapment. Without warning, an unseen hand painted a series of lines, random slashes of black forming squares and rectangles that stretched out into the white ether, forming an event horizon across his field of vision. At the centre directly in front, the lean lines warped into an oval. Desperate fear, an unusual feeling for him, exploded as the oval eye shape became filled with slashes leaning to the left. He tried to flee, to return to the warm confines of his body. Something held him firm, unwilling or unable to let go. He squirmed as the 'eye' pulled him closer, patterns rushing past as he accelerated toward the horizon. The oval transformed from bland black to a terrible harsh orange, the colour of an alien sun. Its heat seared his incorporeal form before he reached it. Agony consumed Lucent as the 'eye' closed in and embraced him, slamming him back into his soaked writhing body. The burning torment lasted for days, defying all medical treatments. All the balms, lotions and arcane *magicks* were useless. Lucent bore it, even as the fire burned into his bones.

He was a slow learner however. The pain subsided, the burns healed and he tried to kill again. And again. Each time, the pain increased, lasting longer, searing deeper until he begged for death. The fourth attempt was enough to convince the killer to comply. He was a prisoner. He had to accept this reality. Healed and compliant, Phillipe offered him a small crumb of information couple with a characteristic threat.

"The Intercessionary works well, I see. Our little insurance against your prodigious…talent. And if you ask who or what the Intercessionary is, I'll remove one of your balls. With my teeth."

Lucent settled into captivity, making do with extreme porn, the jazz stylings of John Coltrane and his visits to the Killing Room. His 'gambols', as he liked to term them, provided him with the excitement of the kill, all state-sanctioned and above board. He was doing a public service. Phillippe said so.

The corridor straightened out. At the far end stood a tall stocky man, his white smock a stark contrast against his dark skin. Hands clasped behind his back, the man did not move or speak, only stared with dead eyes. *Moritz*. Lucent's cheer dissolved at the sight of the solid Fijian. There was no love lost between the two. There was never any love to begin with.

Love.

More of a word than an emotion in the modern age. It was a slippery concept in a world devouring itself slowly, fracturing along lines created by agenda and dogma. Race, religion, politics, taste; these things and more had become more important than simple love and respect. Maybe the time had come for this world to end. Kayvan sighed, a sad sound muffled by the chorus of jeers and shouts below. He swigged from the still cold bottle, settling in for the entertainment. Below, the main road had cleared. Shoppers, criminals, pensioners had either fled into the nearest building for safety or remained propped up against filthy windows, eagerly anticipating the bloodshed to come. The Limbostani Barmy Army took no prisoners, especially when the intruders were the more religiously minded zealots of the Aston Afterlife *Fauj*.

Squaring up against each other, the groups hurled insults, songs, chants and bottles.

"We're the Barmy Limbostani

La-lalala."

"You're such a loverly bunch of coconuts,

Kissing the main man's fat arse"

Despite himself, Kayvan smiled. The causes were different, the end result the same. Young men liked to fight. It had been the same in his youth, it was the same today, despite the *Public Gathering and Public Offence Ordinance*. No laws, no education camps, nothing could stop them. Suppression and the banning of football had only made the problem worse. But here, in the *Limbostan*, out of sight and mind of the *Trendies*, anything went.

Two lads peeled off from their respective groups, sauntering into the glass strewn no-man's land between them. The Aston boy, a white scarf covering his face, pointed a jagged broken bottle at his opponent.

"We're on your manor, you fuckin' Uncle. *Tu kaun ah?* No one, that's who. *Teri bhen dhe lun*, I'll wet you up so bad, that fat financial minister bitch won't want you fuckin' her."

The Limbostani smiled. Face uncovered, head encased in an old baseball cap, he looked all of fourteen. His stance spoke otherwise; of a life of fighting. Reaching into his jacket, he hurried forward. Hesitant, the Aston boy stepped back too late. The

Limbostani pulled a blunt stubby object from his jacket, flicking his wrist to the floor.

"*Raasclart bhenchod, tuwadhi maan nu potch meh kaun hai.*"

A meaty *thwock* filled the air as a telescopic baton hit home. The Aston boy swayed, crumpling to the ground, blood seeping onto concrete. A roar filled the air as the youths piled into each other with venom.

Passers-by swerved around the conflagration, looking down or looking away, not wanting to incur the wrath of youth. If the kids wanted to kill each other, let them. They had their own problems to deal with.

The brawl sputtered out within moments leaving two motionless on the floor. Their cohorts offered no help, both sides sauntering off, hands in pockets, swapping battle stories as they melted away. The casualties remained where they fell, blood leaking from wounds, leeching into the greedy hot tarmac. The spectators, sated by the violence, dispersed, offering no help, only furtive gloating glances. Live or die, life in the Limbostan thundered on, relentless and unforgiving.

Kayvan straightened up, guilt gnawing at him, common sense prevailing. Offers of assistance could be construed as taking sides. He had enough trouble in his life without inviting the wrath of the gangs. He took another deep drink, casting his gaze out cityward. Cast against the hazy ochre of the August afternoon, skeletal frames of new buildings dominated the skyline, a parade of half-finished citadels promised to the rich and the righteous, a painful reminder of a past sundered, a future denied. Kayvan Singh Katori had been a member of the great and the good, moving from a humble start in one of the many 'Suburbistans' flanking the glittering city heart. His art had been a passport in those days, allowing him fast-track access to a world previously hinted at on flat screen. Everything was in the palm of his hands.

His stubborn honesty to himself hastened his descent from darling of the Master Class to another loser in The Limbostan. Love wasn't the only thing to be killed off in the Brave New World. Humour and independent thought were also lined up against the wall and despatched.

The cleansing by the Style Guardians had been insidious and rapid. Dissent and rebellion awoke too late to stop the movement. Art was a sterile affair now, committee-approved and thoroughly sanitised; lucrative if you played your cards right, deadly if you persisted. Others like him, mavericks unwilling to submit and be subsumed, either exiled themselves to The Limbostans as he had done, vanished totally or ended up bound and mutilated in high profile locations. Art become deadly to the creators. At the very least, he still breathed, and he still created. The gift he had been given was too deeply ingrained, to ignore or sterilise

We were caught napping, he thought sourly.

Twilight coloured the fringes of the day, motes of sunlight bouncing off the white marble onion dome of the nearby Gurdwara. A line came to him from the Guru Granth Sahib, unbidden:

"There are nether worlds beneath nether worlds and hundreds of thousands of heavenly worlds above."

The words, as holy as they were, induced a thrill of horror within him. Guru Nanak's theory was innocent enough; Earth was not the only reality in an infinite Universe. It was the 'nether worlds' that unnerved him. He had seen them, in dreams and in hints of everyday life. He divined certain events, saw certain people, understood danger and safety. Through his art, he tried to warn of tyrants, of men and women offering benediction and solution whilst waiting for their time to destroy. He had foreseen the death of his wife, the coming of the New Flesh, even the beginnings of the new 'Smiling Men' Law Enforcement initiative. Attempting to pass this off as satire and critique, Kayvan came under ever-increasing fire from critics, media and government officials. A fire at his town house was the last straw. Unscathed but frightened, he fled, making his way to the Handsworth Limbostan under cover of darkness and the protection of Krazy Kwezi, a former Doom Rapper.

He was safe enough here. No police ventured into the Limbostans now ubiquitous in most cities. If they did, they never returned. The Limbostan was fast becoming the refuge for all and a symbol of defiance. Faces became known and accepted enough for the unfamiliar to draw attention. Nothing was a secret in the Limbostan unless you requested it.

"Eh! Artist. Yeah, you mad *modda-fukka.*"

Jarred by the loud sonorous voice, Kayvan looked down at the shouter.

"Kwezi," Kayvan responded. "What do you want, *mizungo?*"

Kwezi beamed, his smile honest and good-natured, even though he had been insulted. Easy banter went down well in The Limbostan, if certain lines were not crossed. It was a rule adhered to by all, regardless of race, religion or orientation.

"How's the paintings?"

Kayvan shrugged, wiggling his hand in a 'so-so' gesture. "Could be better. Could be worse."

"No, you melt," Kwezi replied, still smiling. "Those paintings you got from the Frog."

Kayvan nodded his understanding, feeling a little foolish. Kwezi had put him in touch with a local art seller, Herve Fournier. Kayvan came away, lighter in the pocket but owning some new art to cover holes left in the rotting plaster of his new home.

"I've got them up. He's an… interesting guy."

An understatement. Fournier jumped at every sound, every shadow. His eyes skittered, a tic that gave the Frenchman the look of a man about to crack. He had demanded to see several pieces of identification, turning surly and unhelpful until Kwezi threatened to burn the building down. Fournier was obviously a man in hiding, paranoid and secretive.

Kwezi laughed, the sound echoing around the darkening street. "You don't know the half of it, mate. Froggy Fournier's no Limbostani. He's too white…sorry, too *mizungo*. He's only here because of politics. Same as most of us"

Kayvan nodded. He could relate.

A foreboding thunderhead rolled over the Centre, purple tongues of lightning firing randomly. Even the weather had become brutal and harsh, absorbing the cruelty below, spitting it back down as if the taste was too rancid

"It's coming in quick, Kwezi. Better fuck off indoors sharpish."

Kwezi made a dismissive gesture, puffing his cheeks. *"Fock dat modda fukka.* What's a storm gonna do with Crazy Kwezi, eh? *La Negre Invincible*, you feel me?"

With that, Kwezi headed off towards a decayed-looking pub on the corner. Kayvan watched the dreadlocked man weaving his way through the smattering of shoppers and commuters, hailing familiar faces. The sky shook as the storm drew closer, scattering the crowd below. As he returned to the dry comfort indoors, he felt a slight lurch in perception, as if time and space had slipped a groove. He glanced over his shoulder at the darkening sky, confused and a little afraid. The thunderhead resembled a skull picked clean, grinning with mirth and malice. Kayvan slid the door shut on the storm but the alienation and fear clung to him long after the rains began to lash at the glass.

The tranquiliser was ice cold. Lucent did not complain. The chilled sedative felt as familiar to him as his own blood. Relaxing, he exhaled, quivering as the drug stroked his nervous system. In the corner of his eye, Moritz hovered, all muscle and violence. Lucent could almost smell the hate leaking from his pores; a bland copper odour. Swivelling his head, Lucent gazed at the man, briefly considering a smile, thinking better of it.

Lucent may have been Phillipe's star prize but he wasn't precious enough not to let the Fijian slap him about a bit if needed. His eyelids began to droop, the drug taking hold. Phillipe's voice rang in his mind, echoing and a little indistinct. Summoning the last of his strength, Lucent turned to look at his jailer hovering over him.

"Are you ready to give the artist our gift?"

Tongue too thick to allow speech, Lucent nodded.

"Excellent. Artists should be seen and not heard. He was warned, time and time again. Yet even from hiding he finds ways to be… uncooperative. If he is so unhappy with the burden of living, we'll give him the gift of ending it for him. A cruel gift, but the man seems to be suffering." Phillipe loomed above him, amphibian features leering. Lucent noticed flecks of white foam gathering at the corners of his jailer's mouth. His stomach lurched.

"Well, you seem to be ready to depart. The Intercessionary will guide you, as always. Good luck and good hunting."

Air left Lucent's lungs in a dry heave as a wave of sedative pulled him into the ether. His eyes closed, his face becoming slack and doughy with a hint of a grateful smile. His freedom may have been limited but it was still freedom after a fashion. It was still a gift to cherish.

Kayvan's arms spasmed. Licking dry lips, he let them drop into his lap, his head bowing. The canvas was heavier than it looked. Thunder rumbled, closing in fast. The noise was muted by the sibilant sound of John Coltrane blaring from tatty speakers. Jazz aided concentration and introspection, he found. Shifting from buttock to buttock, he raised the picture once more, focusing on the image and the music. The artwork was one of three identical pieces he had bought from Fournier's tatty shop on the main street. The skittish Frenchman may have been paranoid and twitchy but when it came to payment, he became cool and clinical, relieving Kayvan of his money with a flourish and a receipt. Business was not booming by the wasted look of Fournier's face. Limbostans did not seem to favour the arts, unless it was music. Bad music, at that. The last craze, a hybrid of Polka and Lover's Rock, ruled the Handsworth airwaves, a mash-up that jarred the senses at a base level.

Kayvan grabbed the heavy bundle, exiting the stale shop, puzzled at this purchase. The art was not to his taste. It was too stark, clean-cut and monochrome. A few curves broke the rigidity of the piece, particularly in the centre where the spread of square and rectangle met, warping into a concave line filled iris. But, beyond that, the painting was harshly neat and symmetrical. Stray pentagons, top and bottom, were the only unusual feature, eye-catching in the thickness of their form and difference to the linoleum stretch of squares.

The piece caught his eye, compelling him to study it further as he had rushed back indoors away from the storm and the hallucination of the skull. That's all it could have been. It could not have been a portent; he had not dreamt of such a thing. The creature and his card-playing victim had been the last vision he had, although he was unsure what that was a harbinger of. Maybe the strain was finally catching up with him. Living on the run, ostracised and threatened, took a toll sooner or later.

The three copies occupied a wall each, two facing each other, the last one hanging on its own. He had ensured that they lined up perfectly, a concession to aesthetics, obsessive compulsiveness and something less definable but akin to safety. There was a talismanic quality to these simple pieces of line art, a sense that they were more than just product.

Once he had calmed down, grabbed some more beer and selected mood music, Kayvan grabbed the nearest canvas and sat. An hour on from that moment and he was still none the wiser. No great revelation had been gleaned from staring at the picture. His eyes were hot, his arms stiff and his sanity questioned. The picture remained the same and no insights had been forthcoming.

Thunder crashed. Startled, Kayvan dropped the picture, the thud of its frame masked by the boom. The windows rattled but held firm. Breathing hard, he stood. His skin rippled with loathing, gooseflesh rippling his arms. Thunder crashed once more. The lights and John Coltrane stopped, plunging the stale-smelling room into a soupy murk. He froze, eyes swivelling frantically as they adjusted to the gloom. Hush descended. It absorbed the thudding of his galloping heart, rendering the silence almost total. Outside sounds were muffled, distorted by a heavy stillness in the air. Kayvan felt dislocated, removed from the Limbostan by a few feet but far enough to be cast out from the world. Fear, filth-stained and cold, coiled around him. Someone else was in the room. The presence was malign, streaked with the malicious joy of a broken clown. Kayvan's throat, dry and shrinking, closed as he tried to talk.

"Who's there?" he croaked, feeling ridiculous. That never worked in the horror films of his youth. What would be so different now? Fighting the urge to speak again, he looked around slowly.

A shadow stood in the doorway, framed by a soft azure glow. Rocking on the balls of his feet, Kayvan swivelled until he was sideways on, presenting less of a target for the intruder. The soft radiance became sharper, stronger, bathing the stranger. Kayvan's lips froze in a snarl of horror, his brain struggling to cope with the oddity before him.

The thing was humanoid in form, sexless and slender. Its skin rippled with colours rotting and foul, colours that he could not name but were familiar from his visions. It had no face, only a blank sheeny surface that sucked light into it. The Mirror Man tipped its head to the side. Kayvan's throat dried a little more as he realised that the thing was studying him.

Moments passed, man and Mirror Man regarding each other, awaiting the next move. The space between them hissed with electrons, the stink of ozone catching the back of Kayvan's already dry throat. Thunder rolled. A baby wailed its distress, accompanied by a chorus of dogs, the discordant sound almost unholy. Delicately, the Mirror Man stepped forward. Kayvan willed his legs to move. His parched throat closed a little more, breath wheezing from him asthmatically.

The Mirror Man raised a fingerless hand. Kayvan watched in abject horror as the hand elongated, flattening and tapering to a point. Golden light glinted from the blade's edge.

"This is going to hurt so much."

Kayvan started at the sound of its breathless voice. It had the light air of a carefree woman, excited by the prospect of an unexpected gift or a lover's touch. Raising the blade, the Mirror Man skipped forward playfully, its free arm swinging by its side. To Kayvan's horror, it giggled, covering its chin with the free hand in a coy gesture.

"Aren't you excited? I am. I get to give you a gift. You get to receive my gift. We're all winners today." In the blink of an eye, the Mirror Man gripped Kayvan's ear, twisting it and pulling him closer to the tip of the blade. Metal filled the artist's vision, a slight sting bringing water as the tip rested on his eyeball. It giggled once more before humming a discordant tune. Kayvan gritted his teeth as the pressure increased.

I will not scream, you bastard. I will not scream.

A yell pierced the foetid air.

Lucent's ethereal form was a secret kept from Phillipe, Moritz and Inquisitors alike.

He killed for them. How he performed and how he did it was not something his captors needed to know. Practice and visualisation solidified this facet of his talent, made the act personal. He thrilled at the feel and touch of victims; the heat of running blood, the gelid sensation of ruptured organs between hands fashioned from thought alone, the orgasmic joy of plunging his head into dripping cavities devoid of their contents. Remote killing - combustion, vein bursting, heart squeezing - had its uses when time was short or a backlog needed clearing. Such methods left him jaded however. The sense of dislocation when his mind was free of form also made him nervous. The fear of drifting beyond reach whilst untethered from the physical haunted him. Physical form comforted.

The bloodlust roared through him, making his ethereal ripple in anticipation. Surveying his prize, he felt a slight disappointment. Phillipe's description of the man had painted a fearsome fire breathing dissident, a man so dangerous that extra-judicial killing was too good for him. This artist – this Kayvan – looked uninspiring and insipid, a study of the mediocre far from the 'enemy of the state' category bestowed upon him. The man was tall, of average build, head shaved fashionably bald. His limbs were long, ungainly as if they had been added as an afterthought. His demeanour reeked of fear and confusion, round face pinched, sweating and nervous.

Lucent questioned Phillipe's assessment of this man. This was no frothing red-eyed revolutionary, all blood, thunder and insurrection; he drew pictures. Offensive, to be sure, but nothing that really called for his destruction. Before Phillipe had strapped him into the chair, Lucent perused the target's back catalogue, scrutinising every brush stroke and shadow.

He knew nothing of art. Cubism, Futurism, it all seemed pretentious and shallow. In his old life, before capture, he remembered a furore kicking up about an unmade bed being exhibited in the Tate Modern. The idea that this was an art piece offended him so much that he tracked down the culprit and burned her from the inside, slowly. It took her three days to be reduced to ash. The wait was worth it. Oh, how she screamed.

Kayvan was different. There was a raw honesty to his work. His commitment to himself showed through every piece. This was a man who would not compromise his vision, whatever the cost. One piece gripped Lucent: a canvas depicting a Lucifer, like the Fallen One of myth yet subtly different, more human somehow. The red-horned Lord dominated the Speaker's Chair of Parliament, one arm draped insolently over the arm rest. He was naked, his rippling torso gleaming. A lengthy member jutted out from his groin, veined with black. With his other hand, he beckoned at the line of unclothed humanity before him, the great good of the land, man and woman, all oiled and ready for him. At the head of the queue, the Prime Minister, grey-haired and bedraggled, his beard patchy, reached down to caress Lucifer's Glory. His eyes shone with devotion, forehead creasing the hammer and sickle tattoo carved from his skin. The leader of the Opposition positioned herself behind the Minister, tongue lolling and ready. The piece, named 'The Price of the Mighty', seduced Lucent's uncultured eye. Every scar, every pucker, every crevasse had been lavishly rendered in a way that made the painting hyper-realistic. Lucent did not need his snuff porn that afternoon. The painting ignited him enough.

A shame. This man has talent. But a kill is a kill.

He stepped forwards carefully, familiarising himself with the feel of this new form, catching himself as he nearly toppled sideways. Laughter welled up within him. He quelled it, not wanting to ruin the intimidating effect of his mirror form. A minor thought transformed his hand, rills of pleasure running through his arm as it become a blade. This new body did not have a heart but he felt the quickening pulse anyway, more of a memory than a sensation. Lucent raised the blade. The left eye first, he decided. The springy feeling, giving way to a *pop* as the eyeball burst was a good way of starting off.

"This is going to hurt", he said. "A lot."

Kayvan's eyes widened with fear. The artist was paralysed, unable to even twitch.

Making it easy for me? I thank you. It won't end quickly though.

A searing pain shot through his left foot. He yelled out, startled and surprised. The knife tip remained where it was, the point indenting the delicate flesh. The pain not abating, Lucent looked down, the blue glow from his body brightening the floor. Confused, he stared a little longer. He was stood on a white canvas, decorated with black lines and shapes. His bewilderment increased. It was a painting, a mere painting. Shifting his balance to his other leg, Lucent pulled his left foot up. The canvas came with it, stuck to his sole. Confusion turned to fear.

The lined shapes of the work began to shift, stretching upward from the white surface, looping around his foot. As they tightened into a restraining grid, an orange glow radiated from within. Lucent hollered once more, the heat sizzling through his shadow form. Fighting panic, the shadow-Lucent dived to the centre of the room, kicking a table to try and dislodge the painting. It was no use, the grid tightening even further, cutting deep into him.

"What have you done?" he screamed at the dazed artist, as a new pain assailed his wrists and throat. The burning was unbearable.

Kayvan watched, mouth hanging open in fascination and horror, as Fournier's trio of monochrome art transformed. The Mirror Man kicked over his table, sending beer bottles flying. The painting stuck fast. In his peripheral, the wall blazed, a burnished orange painful to the eyes and teeth. Like their counterpart, both paintings reconfigured, squares and rectangles flattening into thick coils of amber that burst from the glowing white surface. The tentacles of light lashed around the Mirror Man's limbs. They tightened, suspending him in mid-air. Kayvan coughed at the stink of ozone and blood, his chest convulsing as dry heat leeched his lungs of moisture. Hand over his eyes, he backed toward the door. The Mirror Man loosed a furious scream and curse as the ropes of light pulled and ignited.

Kayvan turned and bolted down the hallway, aware of the fabric melting into his back as the harsh desert-orange light pursued him. Screaming, he threw the front door open and bolted down the piss-drenched hallway, finally collapsing as he reached the street below. Steam wafted from his raw weeping back but the rain quenched the blaze, washing charred fabric away. A hand stroked the back of his bare head as he shut down, hoping the pain would not pursue him into the night.

Phillipe did not react, even as red steam seeped from Lucent's pores. The unconscious killer bucked and writhed, red welts forming on wrists and ankles. The killer's skin sagged, becoming paper-thin and tearing. Moritz tutted as flesh sloughed from bone, hitting the floor wetly. Lucent fell apart without a murmur, his physical being unravelling and spilling itself around him, life-blood pattering as it rained from weakened vessels.

"Moritz."

"Sir." The Fijian's voice was clogged with bile as the ripe odour of internal workings permeated the air.

"Get a clean-up crew please. I have no stomach for it."

Moritz hurried away, fighting the bile rising in his throat.

Mindful of the pools of blood and rapidly liquefying flesh, Phillipe tip-toed closer to the remains of his best weapon. A sick damp odour – part marsh gas, part meat – oozed from the dripping corpse. Phillipe blanched as an eyeball popped audibly, adding its own perfume to the air.

"Mustn't be too disheartened," he murmured to himself. "This *thing* has gained freedom. Of a sort. In death, there are no shackles or Intercessionaries. A cruel gift indeed." In reply, a large chunk of leg muscle unfastened, hitting the ground with a wet splat.

Seeing enough, Phillipe walked away, leaving Lucent's corpse alone, abandoned, eviscerated.

Surrounded.

L. Butcher 2012.

Why didn't I notice that before?

Kayvan shrugged, wincing as a blister opened on his back. Ignoring discomfort, he concentrated on rehanging the picture that had saved his life. A sticker on the back caught his attention. The work had a name after all and a creator. More questions surfaced in his mind. What did the name signify? Who had the artist been surrounded by? Did he or she even live? Fatigue gnawed at him. For now, the answers to these questions would keep. He needed to rest, heal and prepare to leave his new home eventually.

They had found his sanctuary. To remain in The Limbostan would be to invite his own demise. He was certain of that. For now, he remained hyper-vigilant and ready for anything. Krazy Kwezi and his little posse would watch carefully, looking out for any unusual faces. It wasn't much but it would do.

Surrounded.

In a sense, he was. Friends, enemies and others, they all swirled around his orbit, locked in by invisible lines and grids erected for a purpose unknown. Perhaps that was what this Butcher meant? Perhaps not. Another yawn forced his jaws wide open. Kayvan lay chest-down on the old sofa, propping his head up with a cushion. Tiredness took him, surrounding him with dreams of a white landscape, grids, squares, pentagons and the hint of a screaming visage trapped beyond.

Outside, The Handsworth Limbostan moved on, surrounded by the glitter of the city, the stench of the slum.

Clay's Afterword

"A confession. I know next to nothing about art. I'm one of those guys who, when asked their opinion on something remotely arty, will shrug their shoulders, mutter "Errr, its ok", then go back to doing whatever it was I was doing at the time. I'm no heathen but I'm no expert. Art didn't figure much in my upbringing.

"When my friend and all round good chap, Jonathan Butcher asked me if I'd like to contribute to this anthology, I snapped his hand off (figuratively, of course). The chance to be in a collection with names who I know and respect is always a big draw and I was up for a challenge. 'The Cruellest Gift' has been one of the most challenging pieces I've written to date, mainly down to my lack of art expertise. I have no idea what style the piece 'Surrounded' is. I was struck, however, by the boldness and the clash between black and white. Staring at it for hours (as Kayvan, the protagonist, does), didn't quite have the effect of inspiration I'd hoped but it did give me the idea of art as an 'other-wordly' prison or trap. I also thought of using the artwork as a prop to the story rather than the focus. And off I went.

"This tale fits in with my usual 'society gone weird, people gone weirder' schtick and I'm sure that Kayvan, Krazy Kwezi and Phillipe will return at some point in the Clay canon. Oh, and anyone familiar with my work may notice a cameo from one of my own creations. There will be no prize for spotting it all.

"Anyway, please enjoy this tale. I know I did."

It Sucks When You're All Seeds and No Feathers

Duncan P Bradshaw

No way, I got me a visitor! You're not one of *them*, are you? I'm feeling pretty empty inside, so I don't think you're going to get much out of me this month. Sorry.

Oh, you're not. That's a relief.

Hang on, if you're not one of my forebears, you're going to be one of the others, huh? I'm guessing you're here to jackhammer me into mulch with your beak? Looking to bring the curtain down on my excuse of a life and grant me the sweet, sweet embrace of death.

Come to think of it, that'd be quite nice actually. I don't mind if you want to?

No?

I won't say anything.

Nope. Not a peep.

It's not as if you can see my eyes properly either.

You won't feel too guilty or anything.

Go on.

No?

Ah well, you can't blame me for trying.

So you're not what I was expecting, some kind of tourist then, huh? Apologies for my somewhat depressing demeanour and introduction, but hey, look at me! I don't exactly have much going for me these days. In fact, the only thing I do have, is a whole lot of pondering over my life choices. Some might say I have too much time on my hands, but it's been a few years since I've seen them to know that I ever had any in the first place.

That's a joke.

Or an attempt at one.

You'll get it.

Eventually.

Anyhoo…

Given my predicament, I don't really get to go out to many social gatherings these days. Even with all this quality 'me time' going on, I only really have one thought. A recurring nightmare if you will.

How the hell did it get to this?

I've spent most of my life blaming the obvious things, but I think when I get down to brass tacks, take a long hard look in the mirror - a metaphorical one, I'm not afforded such luxuries in my lofty, but shit-encrusted position - I have to admit that perhaps I let things get too far.

Instead of embracing my uniqueness, I took the alternate path, the other option in the Choose-Your-Own adventure book you get dished out to you on Day One of existence. I suppose it all stems from another, albeit simpler question. I'm gonna ask it, and please, give me an answer.

Say it out loud, my earholes may have grown over, but I don't get many visitors out this way anymore, so even the rumbling of your voice will be something.

Go on, give it a go.

For me?

Yeah, I know, I'm a complete stranger, but I'll give you some background info, and you can make your own mind up.

Deal? Okay, so here goes…

Do you know what it's like to be different?

I'm not talking 'one odd sock' different, or 'a wacky sense of humour' different. I'm talking full-blown, one hundred and eight percent different. Can't blame this one on genes, it's not my parent's fault, least not the ones who raised me. I think they were as surprised as anyone when it happened. When I popped out of mama, most of the attendant's first thoughts were less, "Isn't that a cute little baby?" and more, "I wonder if I could eat it before the parents notice."

You see, I'm not like everyone else. Not even close. In a world of beaks, feathers and caw-caws, I'm an abomination, an aberration, I'm pretty much the boogeyman round these parts, even more so after recent events. But right off the bat, from day one of existing in Bird City, I was an outsider. What is it about me that makes the other birds cover their chicks' eyes when I go a-strolling by? Is it my cavalier attitude? The way my face portrays no emotion? Maybe the utter contempt I hold for all of them, following a lifetime of mickey-taking and near constant jibes?

No.

I think the most obvious thing is the bright orange skin. That's a dead giveaway. In this sprawling metropolis of birds, I'm a bonafide, one-of-a-kind, pumpkin man, with pumpkin skin limbs and a carved pumpkin for a head. Where my beak should be, is some weirdass carved hole which passes as a mouth. My eyes, instead of being ideal for spotting breadcrumbs at two hundred paces, are round pitted circles, with no ability to blink or squint.

When I was a young root vegetable, innocent in the ways of the world, I wondered why the other kids in my class would look at me as food, not a friend. My first Feather Preening teacher, Mister Chirpy-Chirpy-Cheep-Cheep, had to be relieved of his duties, due to pecking away on my head as we were all cooped up on a rain break.

None of the other chicks wanted to play with me. As they tucked into their lunchtime millet, I'd sit alone in the corner of the feeding platform, looking down at my lunch, a carton of puddle water, wondering why I was the odd one out.

Why weren't there others like me in school?

Heck, why weren't there others like me anywhere?

Granted, I only left the city twice, each time a field trip upstate to the breadcrumb factory. But even then, as my classmates flew overhead, me running beneath them, struggling to keep up, I only saw a few cats, a dog with a lazy eye and a pack of feral cream crackers. Not once did I see a fellow pumpkinhead roaming around, filled with the same questions, and building resentment as me.

What's that?

I don't seem angry?

I guess that's the benefit of time passing by, plus, what good is it going to do me now?

Some kind of Zen bullshit or something I've built up over the years probably.

Anyway, so yeah, I was bullied. You'd have seen me, if you were covered in feathers and had to perch next to me in morning assembly, wouldn't you? You name it, I had it done to me. Bottom halves of still wriggling worms left in my locker. My giant orange noggin was perfect for being shat on from great heights. My tactile sensitivity got worse with age, and one day I got home to find that the other chicks had painted a dartboard on the back of my head, and I was peppered with balls of dried spit and paper.

It got so bad that my folks, a pair of Cormorants, were called into school. Even through the closed door, I heard the Headmaster, a stern crow by the name of CaCaw Brigstocke, ask my parents to consider moving me to a special school. My father, a proud bird, with a calm reserve not found in his breed, stood up, and said, "Good sir, you will look after my son as if he were the most noble of swans, for if any harm should befall him, then I will make sure that the only roost you have is in a ditch, far from the lofty pylons and electrical wires which criss-cross our mighty city."

I have no idea why he said that, as father worked as a lowly rock pecker in the quarry. The only real thing he was in control of was tapping on the dinner bell twice a day. Suffice to say, from that day forth, it was not only my fellow pupils who now used me as a punchbag, but the teachers too. My English teacher began to conduct lessons solely in the song of the swallow. Science lessons were held atop the tallest lamppost. Sure, I had hands and legs, but my skin was so smooth…so slippery, by the time I managed to get to the top, the class would fly away and relocate to the next spire. Forever was I trying to learn knowledge, but it was always denied to me.

The trickle of hate turned into a torrent, gradually wearing away at the dam of patience within my very being.

Something had to give.

Finally, one night, as we sat down for dinner - which consisted of a two-day-old bagel, father's favourite - I asked the single question that had been burning so brightly within, a metaphorical version of the flaming candle Mrs Tweety had put inside of my head earlier that day.

Bitch.

I laid down my specially made spork, turned to mama, and asked, "Mama, why am I different from the other birds? Why do I not have wings, but these stupid stumpy limbs? Why am I able to pick up things using my dextrous fingers? Why do I not rise at four in the morning and sing the song of my people? WHY MOTHER?"

She stopped pecking at a particularly tough piece of bagel, looked once at father, who picked at his dorsal guiding feathers, and said, "I hoped this day would never come. I want you to know that we both love you very much. However, as you've probably noticed by now, you're not like the other boys or girls. You see... one day, I was strutting along the banks of the River Bachik, and I found a bag of strange beans. I should've known better: why would anyone leave a bag of high quality legumes just lying around for any old bird to find? I should've walked away, anything but eat them all in one sitting.

"I woke up the next day to find my belly swollen and tender. I had to sing in sick, the pain was that bad. Your father thought that those beans might've been popcorn. In the quarry, he'd heard stories of pigeons going through baking hot corn fields, eating the swollen kernels which had bloomed like flower heads, which then promptly reacted with their stomach acid and exploded them open from within. He took refuge in the kitchen nest, just on the off-chance.

"A passing doctor bird stopped by, and gave me the news that I didn't think possible. I was pregnant. This was quite the shock, as your father…well…let's just say he suffers from…performance anxiety."

It was at this juncture my father flew off to the local watering hole, The Mucky Human, leaving mama there embarrassed and alone. Before I could even ask about the whole procreation thing, which sounded like jolly good fun, she continued, "Luckily, your father is a good bird, he promised he would take care of me, and you. He had always wanted a little egg to sit on. Except… you never came. Day after day, we waited for you to pop out of my egg bum-bum, but nothing. The medical staff were baffled, eventually insisting that I go and stay in the hospital nest, over on Seagull and Fifth. You know, by the fence factory?

"My belly continued to swell. I had forgotten what my claws looked like. It felt like I was going to burst open. Finally, one day, an autumn morning, I remember it well, as the crops were starting to wither, I felt like I needed a great big poo. But this one felt funny. It felt… solid. I didn't want to push, fearing that my insides would come out, but my mother always told me that if you need to go, go – just fan out your tail feathers so you don't poop on yourself by accident.

"Against every instinct I had, I pushed, and pushed, and pushed. To my relief, instead of an endless torrent of faecal matter, a screaming orange child came out. You. The doctors and nurses opened their beaks, and no noise came out. You filled up the entire nest, your little gross wriggling orange body, those strange arms and legs of yours, fingers and toes. But most of all your head, with two eyes and a mouth carved into the surface. I didn't know what to do, until you looked at me and squeezed my wing tip with your podgy pumpkin-skin fingers. Well... after that? I would've done anything for you."

I commended mama on a wonderful story, but it was still missing one important detail.

How the hell was I made of pumpkin and not a bird? Her answer?

"I guess it must have been radiation or something. Perhaps an evil magpie curse?"

And that was that. I tried to press her for more details, but she never said another word on the subject. Even on her death nest a few years later, as she coughed up blood and bile after that tomcat had caught her and shook her apart like a bluebottle, she said nothing. She stroked my cheek with her blood-caked feathers, winked – though this caused her one remaining eye to fall out – and cawed softly into what passed as my ear.

We dealt with her body the way all birds do, by letting her decompose down on Mulch Avenue. We lay her side by side with her sister, who had died the previous summer after being hit by a stray lightning bolt. Father, already a recluse, turned to drink, fluttering home late at night, intoxicated on fermented berries and sap, smelling of cheap birds and smoke.

But there was a change going on inside me. My skin was getting tougher. The physical attacks by my peers now did me no harm, and caused me no physical pain. Seeing father shun me, I did the only thing I felt I could: I closed my heart, and for the first time in my life looked upon the birds I shared my life with in a new light.

I hated them with every fibre of my being.

I wanted to get my revenge after the years of suffering they had doled out on me, but how? No bird would ever fight another. Even the proper bastardy of the vultures meant that they only feasted on the dead, and found warm meat to be positively disgusting. I knew the cats and snakes would gladly help me, but what the hell does a prepubescent boy with a pumpkin for a head have to offer?

I can answer this one for you with two words.

Fuck.

All.

The cats merely slept through my requests, whilst snakes, the proper venomous ones, tried to bite me, breaking their fangs on my tough skin. They eventually gave up and slithered away back into the undergrowth.

For a moment, I considered about ending it all. I was the only one of my kind. The birds, my supposed kin, treated me like a walking buffet or latrine. The other animals as if I were some kind of novelty, to be pawed, hissed, bitten or barked at.

I trudged over to the top of the tallest cliff, and looked down at the jagged rocks below. How easy it would be, to let the wind topple me from this peak. Deliver me to the granite below, smash my head in and spread my pulp and seed over the grey angular anvil so far beneath me.

Then it hit me.

Seeds.

And not just any.

My seed.

Yes, very funny.

My seed.

Titter away why don't you? I mean, it's only my life story I'm blurting out to you here.

Hang on, don't go.

Please?

You have to understand, that it's not easy sitting here day in, day out, no stimulus, nothing. I came into this world by mama eating errant radioactive and/or cursed beans, which formed me into a bright orange vegetable person of no discernible gender. I've spent most of my life being ridiculed, so I get a little testy. Okay?

Cool.

So, every once in a while, I would have to hack a slightly bigger hole for my eyes and mouth, to counter my growth spurts. I'd use a piece of broken glass and would gouge out my innards, discarding the seeds, feeding them to the sparrows over on Stoop Road, trying to get them to like me.

What if I didn't?

The plan to befriend them hadn't exactly been a roaring success, the blasted things still circled me as I slept, trying to drop small pebbles into my earholes.

I ran home, shimmied up the nest pole, and rooted around in the branches for my bag. I took out the broken piece of glass and scooped out a handful of my head. I rooted through the gunk, and found that I had five seeds, that would do for my little experiment. I hurried over to Mulch Avenue, and beneath the desiccated skeleton of my mother and her family, I thrust them into the earth, which writhed with maggots and feathers.

Every day for a month, I returned, watering them and tending to the soil. It was fertile land, enriched with bone dust which helped to make the soil a verdant field.

Yet after thirty days…nothing. I raised my head to the heavens, lamented my folly, and plotted my path back to the clifftop. As I was about to leave, I felt something grasp my toes. Daring to look down, I saw shiny orange digits, having broken through the top soil, and latched onto my foot. I brushed the dirt away, and lo… just beneath the surface was my son. My firstborn.

Nigel.

As I bent down and pulled him from the ground like a carrot, another hand broke free, then another, and another… from the five, four had survived, and genesis had been effected. I wasn't alone anymore. Yet the venom of loathing still bubbled inside of me, as I knew that I could not allow my offspring to suffer the same indignities that had been meted out to me. So I carried them, one by one, to a cave on the outskirts of Bird City. There, I taught them how to look after their skin, how to read, how to write, to speak, to question the inequities of root vegetables everywhere.

But most of all, I taught them my seething rage at those damn prissy birds.

After every lesson of language, mathematics and physical education, I told them stories of how I had been mistreated. Sure, some of them may have been embellished slightly, but even with my self-imposed exile, my vitriol for those winged bastards had not diminished.

I can still see them all now, row upon row of dead pumpkin eyes looking back at me, then to each other, fists clenched in resistance, eager to right this wrong.

Within a year, our numbers were in the hundreds. Some of my children were gifted engineers, and began to fashion weapons, not just for melee, but projectile too. Soon we had a wealth of swords, clubs, and simple firearms. Along with our loathing for their kind, we would use the one key thing that our creation had gifted us, which those devil birds did not possess.

Opposable thumbs.

The plan was a simple one, for it had to be, we would wait for the migratory period to start, when vast numbers of the populace would seek warmer climes, and we would target key objectives within the city. A crack squad of my children, trained in deadly hand-to-hand combat, and quieter than a flamingo eating spaghetti, would take control of the feeders, down in Central Plaza. At the same time, a similarly discrete force would capture the bird baths, down on Splish-Splash Lane.

Then, with me leading the main bulk of my army, I would march on the seat of power, the White House, originally a brick building, but covered from top to foundation in foul guano. Will these filthy animals ever learn to not poop wherever pleases them?

I surmised my little insurrection would deal with that.

We did not have long to wait, as our metrological centre, set up by my most gifted child, Samantha, detected a severe cold front coming in, which would cause consternation amongst the bird world, and send them to their nests to pack.

I gave the command and readied my forces. It was time. Time to show these heartless harpies who the new dominant species was in this city. The commandos took their objectives with the minimum of effort, catching the guard storks on the hop, figuratively and literally. It was not without bloodshed though, as a number of lairy blue tits, hopped up on fermented blueberry mash put up a fight, albeit briefly, at the bird baths. They were put down quickly, but brutally, the water running red with their blood.

You should've seen the looks on their faces when I marched down Main Street. A few police doves tried to get in our way, but they were dealt with quickly and efficiently. A quick blow round the back of their heads with a club put paid to their protests. The guards outside the White House were too shocked to resist the massed ranks of pumpkin people marching on them. They cooed, opened the gates and flew away to Paradise City, where rumours persisted of lusher lawns and prettier lady avian.

By now, the air was awash with all manner of calls, some I recognised, others a garbled panicked mishmash of noise. One word kept being repeated… Pumpkinhead. Of course they knew my name. In a city of birds, where there's an anomaly sitting in your kid's classes, or using your rest facilities, they knew who I was. They just didn't expect there to be so many of me. The plan had worked, it was as I envisaged, a time of joy, celebration, brief retaliation and then harmony.

Or so I thought.

As we stood at the bottom of the steps to the White House, the President, a sage old owl called Icky Codknuckle, was waiting for us at the summit. His head was doing laps around his neck, making the rest of the cabinet rather dizzy to say the least. Finally, he ceased, as I approached him and his cadre, one step at a time, letting them see the face of the victor.

A single step from the peak, I stopped, already towering over his diminutive form. I had only seen pictures of him from afar, but up close he seemed so regal, I almost changed my mind. But then the years of abuse and pecking brought me back to my senses. I demanded that he and his parliament stand down immediately, as the time of the birds was to be consigned to history.

Codknuckle bowed shallowly, strode forward to meet me, and cleared his throat, preparing to address the crowd which had gathered in the vast grounds below, and the array of perches conveniently placed around the open area. With a voice firm, steady, not showing any sign of fear, he uttered those immortal four words, "I stand here today…"

Then a single shot ran out. Codknuckle's head rocked backwards, a puff of powdered feathers showing the point of impact, his blood and brains spraying over the Chancellor of the Trill Exchequer. Icky's eyes rolled up into his majestic head before he collapsed backwards, dead.

I was as shocked as he, for I had expressly told my fellow pumpkins that no-one should fire if a peaceful outcome was on the cards. I looked at the still twitching body of Codknuckle, and traced the path of the assassin's bullet.

And there he was.

Nigel.

I demanded to know why he had fired his weapon, how he could disobey my orders. He laughed, a single pall of callous cackling, which was joined by the other pumpkins. Nigel shouldered his weapon, and with his podgy fingers, delved around in his mouth cavity, pulling out a chunk of thick skin, which he had obviously cut with a fine blade. The slab of rind fell to the floor, exposing a fanged maw, carved not in my image, but a new one.

One by one, the rest of the pumpkin army pulled out their own pre-sliced mouths, becoming a sea of evil pumpkinheads, looking back at me as if I were the enemy. The Foreign Secretary, a plump near-senile pigeon, tried to waddle back inside. Harriet, one of the newest grown pumpkins was on him in a flash. Following a flurry of wild swipes with a machete, the pigeon was reduced to bloodied ribbons.

I stared down at Nigel, and asked again, why had he gone against my will?

He stomped up the stairs, and stared deeply into my eye cavities. "You taught us to despise them, father. You taught us nothing but hatred, rage and anger. We are made in your own image, are we not? I thought you would be proud. For did we not do this day what you had wished? Isn't this why you grew us all, and nurtured us, so we could exact this just and noble revenge?"

My little pumpkin heart sank. Is this all I had taught them? Murder? I told him and the others, that I did not want this, I wanted the coup to be bloodless, a seamless transition of power from the old to the new. They were nasty to me, yes, but there were moments of occasional compassion.

"Yet you did not teach us this father – you armed us, told us they were the enemy, and marched us to war. Are you really that shocked that we would do this without compunction? Exactly as you had trained us?"

The gathered crowds, both high and low, began to get nervous. The pumpkins turned to regard them, preparing weapons, picking out targets. I knew that what I would do next would be nothing more than a token gesture, a futile exhibition of selflessness which would never be recorded, for history does not remember the vanquished.

I shouted at the birds to flee, to escape this place.

It was too late. Shots rang out. Birds fell from their perches to the ground. The injured were set upon, and killed. Those who did not heed my warning, and did not take to the skies, were swarmed where they stood, and murdered. Within a matter of minutes, every winged creature in that arena was dead or dying.

Nigel, his face streaked with blood, and with a solitary white dove's feather stuck to his head, turned to me, "Oh, father, it seems you do not want this world that we have created." He pulled his sword from its scabbard and lunged at me, removing my head from my torso.

Yet I did not die.

My body was burned, the White House painted anew. A deep crimson, the paint made with the blood of the innocents, as Nigel and his followers, my progeny, swept to power. The birds, not the most intelligent creatures, let's admit it, did not flee, and were enslaved. In schools, a new truth was taught: that they were the subservient ones, and pumpkins were the one true race.

And me?

Well you found me here, didn't you?

My head, all that remains of me, sits in an alcove overlooking Mulch Avenue. My mouth has near sealed over, and no one has bothered to carve it open and free. My eyes, nothing more than two pinpricks in this tough old skin of mine. Nigel cut the top of my head open, and once a month, a ceremony is held where new seeds are pulled from my insides, and sown amongst the ancestral dead of this city, the carrion ranks replenished by the freshly slaughtered.

Now, every bird is clipped at birth to prevent them from flying away, the final *pièce de résistance* of cruelty exacted by my spawn. Too late do I see that I should've taught my offspring to embrace their differences, not to use them as a furnace for hatred.

Every year, on the anniversary of the uprising, at the end of the month of October, pumpkins, grown as they should be in tilled land, are harvested. That terrible ghastly visage of snarled mouths and evil eyes are carved within their flesh. At every junction, and at every residence, they are left out on display, lit from within by a solitary candle to remind the birds who is in control.

I am glad you found me, traveller. But no happy ending do I have for you this day.

If I were you, I would take your leave, before one of the pumpkin militia finds you here, and executes you for sedition.

Unless…

Would you be willing to grant a cantankerous old foolish pumpkinhead one final wish?

It is a simple one.

Climb that cliff, with me in the crook of your arm, back to where I contemplated my end, and cast what remains of me from atop the tallest peak. Let my mulch splatter against the jagged rocks below. Bear witness to the waves carrying my blasted flesh and guts down and out into the depths of the sea.

Maybe there, at the bottom of the ocean, my sacrifice will bear more children.

Yet this time, I hope that whatever remains of me, every remnant or scrap of pulp, seed, memory and regret, will teach them something different.

Something better.

Duncan's Afterword

"The main thing that grabbed my eyeballs first off is the round shape on the left-hand side. It looked like a carved Halloween pumpkin. Initially, I had the idea to do a story based on masked serial killers in a retirement home, but the more I stared at the picture, I picked up other details. There are a few angular beak-like faces, not necessarily straight and level with the pumpkinhead, but swarmed around him. To the right, there is a cylinder which looks like a perch for a budgie in a cage. Then the idea of this strange person, completely at odds with the other inhabitants of the world, hit me. What would it be like for this pumpkinhead to live in a place where everyone either wanted to core him out, or shun him? The first draft was a bit wobbly in tone, being quite jokey up front, but then way too moralistic at the end. It didn't sit right, but when I read it back, I found that the tale of him being the victim of his own choices, and the possibility for redemption, albeit only hinted at, was a pretty cool one, and very much in keeping with the current times Ultimately, like most things, it comes down to a choice. Do you turn the other cheek, embrace your uniqueness and find a way to live, or do you give in to hate and seek revenge on those who you perceive to have wronged you? I love the whole narrator talking to the reader vibe too, used it in a few short stories now, and think it's a good vehicle here in relaying the events of the story."

GROTTO

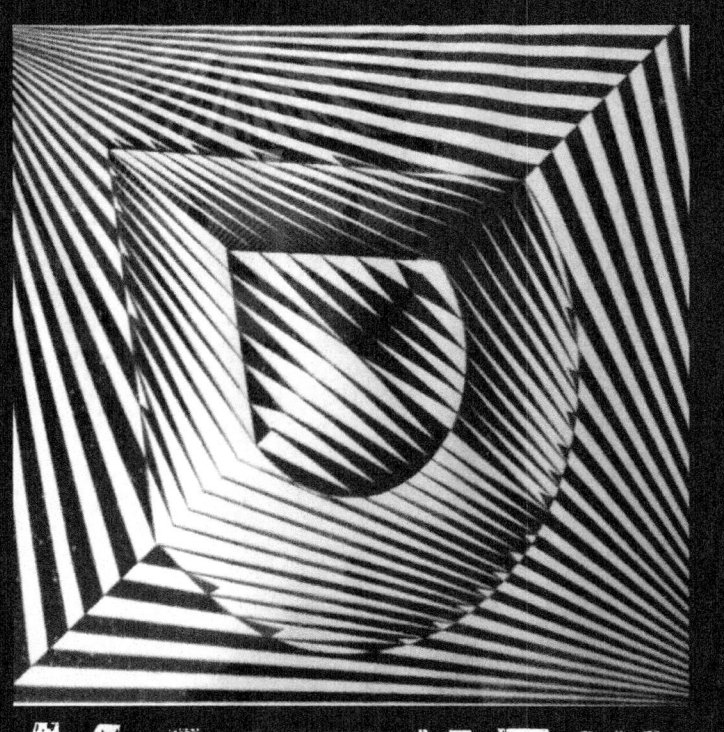

MATTHEW CASH

From the pine-fragranced Cthulhu air freshener that jiggled beneath the rear-view mirror, to the threadbare socks with Christopher Lee's *Taste the Blood of Dracula* inside his black converse, Josh was a complete horror fanatic. Although there was nothing particularly macabre about the red Vauxhall Corsa he drove, his driving was pretty horrific.

"Look, pack it in or else you can wait until we get home to eat," Josh said, scowling in the mirror at the two boys squabbling on the back seat.

"Leave your brother alone David. It's unkind," Nancy said from the passenger side, groggily peering at the grey day outside. The weather had gotten worse the closer they were to the coast, and despite Josh's words of wisdom that coastal weather never lasts, it was persistently proving him wrong.

"Mummm," came a whiny voice from behind Josh. "Dylan just called me a twat!"

"Dylan don't call your brother a twat. You mustn't say that word – it's on the list, remember?" Nancy said, turning to glare over her left shoulder at the older of the two boys.

Dylan, a pimply but preening adolescent, grumbled under his hanging emo fringe but remained glued to his phone.

Observing the heavy rain and thick, ominous dark clouds that appeared in the spaces between the row of three-storey houses, Nancy looked at her husband doubtfully.

"Josh, are you sure it's going to be open in this?"

Josh flicked the windscreen wipers on full and wove the car between the parked cars lining each side of the road. "Course it will, it's inside, innit?"

"You sure they read your email correctly? Because you remember what happened when we went to The Walsall Triangle?"

Josh rolled his eyes and smacked a hand against the steering wheel.

"I read it right. *They* were the ones who had the date wrong."

He scanned the houses they passed. Almost every one was a Bed and Breakfast, and almost every one had vacancies. They tried to glamorise their places by giving them fancy names. They passed Lodges, Guesthouses, and one Inn. Then he spotted a weathered sign at the end and grinned. "Anyway, we're here."

As fortune would have it, there was space for several cars outside the building which housed The Primpton Shell Grotto. Josh pulled into the gap and promptly switched the engine off. "Right," he said turning to his two boys. "Electronics, now!"

David pouted from behind his games console, switched it off and handed it to his dad. Dylan's eyes rolled upwards and after a series of complicated thumb-swipes and tappings he reluctantly passed over his phone. "Let's go see this piece of shit so we can go to Maccies."

Josh snatched the phone from the teenager. "It's not a piece of shit," he said in complete disregard to his wife's list. "It's an ancient, rare archaeological discovery, and one of the wonders of the South East of England."

Dylan pulled a face and pressed the button on his seatbelt.

"That was on the website wasn't it?" Nancy said quietly.

"Yeah," Josh nodded with genuine excitement before jumping from the car and into the pelting rain. "Come on, you won't believe your eyes."

Nancy sighed heavily at the prospect of venturing outside the vehicle. "I'm sure I won't."

The first little worm of uncertainty wriggled its way down Josh's ventromedial prefrontal cortex; the part of the brain that controls belief and doubt. The small, badly-paved path leading to the three-storey house that held the Primpton Shell Grotto was less than impressive. Josh was no DIY enthusiast but could already spot various amendments he would make to the exterior of the building. From what he had learnt from their vastly outdated website they didn't charge an admittance fee and preferred to encourage people to show their appreciation via donations to The Primpton Grotto Preservation Society. It didn't seem like people had been very appreciative of late.

Josh pushed his finger against a cracked doorbell and counted two seconds before a strangulated chime came from inside.

Another few seconds went by before they heard a weird robotic voice flatly telling them to wait.

Nancy looked at her husband with the deepest confusion whilst Dylan smirked and

David stared mouth agape as the door slowly opened.

An elderly man whose head seemed to be comprised of a gigantic pendulous nose and elephantine ears somehow smiled a greeting to them and pressed what looked like an electric shaver to a pouting hole in his throat and spoke.

"Hello, I'm Cuthbert Spencer, you must be the Archers, like the radio show?" He laughed politely, making sure he lowered his electric larynx first.

Josh offered his hand for a shake, and as soon as Cuthbert's back was turned Nancy shot a stern look at her two boys. That look said, "Don't you fucking dare take the piss! One laugh, one smirk, one miniscule titter and you'll have that much confiscated it'll be like living in the Dark Ages!"

The Archers followed the old man's shrunken, stooped figure through a tiled hallway, Josh enthusiastically wittering on about how long he had been wanting to visit the place, Nancy elbowing her eldest in the ribs as he did robot impressions.

Cuthbert stopped by a door beneath a normal-looking staircase. A well-polished gold plaque announced that this was the Primpton Shell Grotto. Josh hid his disappointment well but Nancy saw his shoulders slump as the realisation that he had quite possibly driven them three hundred miles to look at a pile of shit sunk in.

Cuthbert unlocked the door and pressed his talking device against his throat: "Welcome to the Primpton Shell Grotto."

Josh gasped, Nancy gasped and to Josh's utter surprise he actually heard an audible, "Wow," from Dylan, and a "Cool," from David. He swelled with immense paternal pride as he and his family took in the three little wooden steps that led down to a winding stone spiral staircase which looked like it had been carved into the stone walls.

"Careful. Sometimes the steps get slippery," Cuthbert said as he started down.

"Though we are quite fortunate not to suffer from the damp."

As the steps continued their downward spiral, the stone wall became lighter in colour and small scatterings of different-sized shells decorated it intermittently.

Josh gazed up at the crudely-fitted bare lightbulbs that gave just enough light to see Cuthbert's back.

"I bet you are thinking: how many steps?" Cuthbert said. He didn't wait for an answer. "Fifty-five."

Below them the darkness huddled like a physical entity. Cuthbert stopped walking and carefully shuffled around to face them.

Josh could sense a large open space. He drew the zipper of his coat right beneath his throat as the sudden temperature drop hit.

"Welcome…" Cuthbert said for the second time, his free hand fumbling on the wall. "…to the Primpton Shell Grotto."

Strip lighting flickered on, illuminating the subterranean wonder.

Cloisters and archways surrounded them like the interior of an ancient chapel. Everywhere they looked, they were surrounded by shells depicting intricate mosaics and patterns.

Josh looked around, awestruck. From floor to domed ceiling, every surface was decorated with stars, moons, aquatic life, and other unfamiliar symbols, all made with collected shells of all sizes.

A large serpentine spiral covered the room, leading to a roughly cuboid section of rock upon which sat an oval dish that seemed to be comprised of fused-together oyster shells.

Cuthbert smiled at them and raised his device. "In a few moments I'll let you have a good look round in here and the adjoining chambers, but first, allow me to tell you about the Grotto."

Josh squeezed Nancy's hand and was more than happy to see that she was fascinated by her surroundings; a glance at the boys told him that their attention was already waning.

Cuthbert stepped forward into the centre of the shell spiral and pressed the electric larynx to his throat. "The Primpton Shell Grotto is an underground marvel, and one of the wonders of the South East of England."

Josh nudged his wife and whispered, "Told you," into her ear.

"It was discovered in 1879 by my great grandfather whilst he was digging to install a carp pond, but its age remains a mystery," Cuthbert said, and moved over to place a hand on the central piece, the raised rock holding the bowl. "Ninety-nine percent of all surface area is covered in mosaics created entirely of seashells. There are roughly two hundred and forty square metres of mosaic, or over eight million shells. The purpose of the structure is unknown, but theories include an eighteenth or nineteenth-century folly; a garden ornament if you will, or perhaps a prehistoric astronomical calendar. Some," he said, tapping a finger against the oyster shell bowl, "believe it has religious aspects, although what religion has obviously yet to be determined, but my own suspicion is that this was created long before Christianity."

Josh was truly spellbound. It was exactly what he'd hoped it would be, and his brain was whirring with inspiration and creativity. What if this were some ancient forgotten religion?

The most frustrating thing about the place and its history was the fact that there were no answers; nobody knew how long it had gone undiscovered deep within the chalky soil.

He couldn't keep his eyes still, though he hung on the tour guide's every word. He was transfixed by the place. He wanted to study it, poring over every millimetre of the caverns. He was sure that after seeing the place he would discover his own theory as to what it had been built for, and currently favoured the religious idea. He nervously raised a finger to interrupt Cuthbert's monologue. "Umm. Do you think that dish was a font of some kind?"

Cuthbert appeared to ignore Josh's question, "Come closer, if you will." He beckoned Josh over to look into the deep bowl.

The bowl was a thing of beauty, and the way the rough oyster shell exterior had been stuck together and polished down was remarkable. The interior was a smooth, flawless white with a pearlescent sheen when the light caught it. In the centre, there was a hole no bigger than coin.

"Why would a font have a hole in it?" Josh asked, although he knew the answer.

"It wouldn't," Cuthbert said, his rheumy blue eyes glinting. This close, Josh noticed the hole in the man's throat twitch and he tried not to gawp.

"If you pay close attention," the tour guide said, and crouched with surprising agility to the base of the decorative stone plinth. "There are exit holes here." Cuthbert pushed his finger against a trio of tiny holes.

Josh crouched down for a more detailed inspection. The holes were all in a straight line above the start of the floor spiral's outward loop. He touched his finger against it and noticed it was concave, like a gutter. The pattern was formed of runnels of flat oblong shaped shells, as though the whole mosaic was designed to carry whatever fluid was put in the bowl. He gasped when the realisation hit him. He knew exactly what fluid this would be a conduit for.

Cuthbert could tell what he was thinking and grinned at him, nodding.

"Shit," Josh said abruptly, and stood up. "You think this was a sacrificial altar?"

Cuthbert ran his finger around one side of the bowl edge. "If you look closely, you will see that the rim is not an exact oval. In fact, this side curves inward slightly. I think this was a *human* sacrificial altar."

"Jesus!" Nancy muttered.

The boys, up until now lost in a series of obscene gestures they were making at each other, pricked their ears up at the gruesome suggestion.

"Of course," Cuthbert said, and offered a reassuring smile. "Human sacrifice in these times would have been a privilege, as these were specially chosen people, pure, often virginal, and the sole child of a family. They would believe that whatever God they were giving themselves to would reward them for eternity in some ethereal paradise."

"Oh, well that's alright then," Nancy said, smiling awkwardly.

"Anyway, enough theorising. You will be talking about this for years, and I am certain you will have your own interesting ideas. Please feel free to email me them." He turned to Josh. "Let me tell you about the shells," Cuthbert began, but was interrupted by a less than subtle groan from Dylan.

Josh flushed with embarrassment and Nancy shot one of her killer glances at her oldest boy before turning it back to the tour guide as one of apology.

"It's fine, it's fine," Cuthbert said. "I was young once, too." He directed his next words to the boys, "Please, feel free to look around wherever you like whilst I show your parents the other chambers."

Josh stepped away from Nancy and the tour guide and spoke to the boys quietly but harshly. "I can't take you two anywhere! Now shut up or we'll have a salad for dinner."

David's little ten-year-old face was mortified and his mouth gaped in an attempt to protest, but Josh moved away from them.

Dylan watched the tour guide lead his parents through a low archway branching off from the circular room, and stuck his first two fingers up at their retreating backs.

"FUCK YOU," he said, in an imitation of Cuthbert's artificial voice.

David made sure his mum and dad had left the room, and then sniggered.

"What a load of lame shit," Dylan said, flicking his fringe from his eyes and forcing his hands deeper into his pockets.

"Yeah man," David said, mimicking his older brother's gesture.

Dylan scuffed his trainer against a twist of spiral mosaic. "Fucking shell shit."

David laughed again. "Shell shit!"

Dylan smirked, secretly enjoying his younger brother's adoration. He lazily scanned the room and momentarily considered its uses. "Ye olde fucking man-cave."

"But shells, Dyl?" David said, doubtful that there was anything masculine about shells.

"Be cooler with skulls," Dylan said, his eyes glowing. "Like the catacombs in France where there's a billion skeletons beneath the streets."

"Wow, really cool!" David said, picturing the streets of France with skeletons bursting from manhole covers and drains.

"Yeah man, it's where the French put all their dead people. This place would be better made of bones instead of ye oldeman-cave shells." Dylan moved across the room to the raised rock that the oyster bowl rested on. "Sacrifice, my arse," he muttered, looking into the hole in the bowl's centre. A mischievous grin came to his face. "I know what this used to be."

"What, Dyl?" David whispered, and then slapped his hands over his mouth as his big brother undid the fly of his jeans.

"A urinal," Dylan said, and shot a thick stream of piss into the oyster bowl.

"The majority of the shells used throughout the Grotto are locally-sourced mussels, cockles, whelks, limpets, scallops, and oysters," Cuthbert continued, showing Josh and Nancy a small, strangely triangular room. When they had come into the room, Cuthbert had immediately warned them of the poor lighting and a hole to one edge of the ground. An orange road cone looked out of place standing by it. He raised a finger up to a large mural of what appeared to be an octopus or jellyfish and pointed to the dirty white shells in between its tentacles. "Most of the white backgrounds to these pieces are made from flat winkle shell, which is..."

"What's down there?" Josh rudely interrupted. He knew it was the wrong thing to do but curiosity had gotten the better of him.

"Ah my dear boy, I see some of the explorer in you." Cuthbert said, smiling widely.

"Now I wouldn't normally do this, and this is top secret information, but I've held my tongue too long, and no doubt it'll be open to the public soon enough." Cuthbert moved over to the edge of the hole and pushed the road cone aside. "I believe," Cuthbert said, with childish excitement, "That I have discovered another level of the Primpton Shell Grotto!"

Josh's eyes went wide. "How the hell did that happen?"

Cuthbert was silent for a moment and his smile faded. "I was a little clumsy a few weeks ago, with a hammer." It was a terrible lie and one Nancy and Josh saw through immediately.

"Now, I don't know how to go about it but if you have a lighter, or maybe a light on your phone, you can have a look inside."

Nancy shook her head; there was no way she was crawling around in here.

Josh snatched his phone from his pocket and nearly blinded Cuthbert with the hellishly bright torch beneath the camera lens. He got to his knees and shone the light into the hole.

A drop of about four feet showed debris from the fallen chalk and something else directly below. "There's something in there," he said, and flattened to his stomach.

"Really?" Cuthbert said, peering into the hole, "I've not been able to investigate further as yet." He gestured to the aperture. "Please. If you can reach it."

Josh shuffled forwards on his elbows and saw that the hole was more than wide enough for him to fit his head and shoulders into. He thrust his arms into the hole and slithered half inside.

The interior was a small space, possibly big enough for one person to sit comfortably in, like a cubby hole or den. Josh gasped.

"What is it? What is it?" Cuthbert said, forgetting to use his device. His voice was a withered dry rasp.

Josh pushed himself out of the hole, his hair powdered with dust, and handed something to Cuthbert.

"Oh, that's beautiful." Nancy said, admiring the large conch shell Josh had found.

Cuthbert fell onto his backside staring at the shell in his hand, the electric larynx forgotten on the floor, his head shaking in disbelief. "My God!"

"What is it?" Josh said, studying the oddly-coloured shell. It was impenetrable black, curving inwards to a dark bloody red. Thin vein-like patterns bled from the opening.

"Is it rare?" Nancy chirped in eagerly. "Valuable?"

"Priceless," Cuthbert rasped through his ruined voice box. He clutched the conch in one shaking hand whilst he retrieved his talking device and attempted to snap out of his daze. "What else is down there?"

Josh lowered himself back into the hole headfirst. He shone his phone's torchlight around the small space. Obscure paintings covered the smooth light stone walls, which he mentally corrected as he hung upside down. "Weird stuff. There's what looks like pictures of people being sacrificed." He studied the strange runes painted everywhere and, knowing he couldn't decipher them, just focused on the art. "And some weird gods or something."

"Describe the gods," Cuthbert said.

Josh felt the man shake him impatiently. Above a group of worshippers stood a vaguely humanoid fish-thing; bulging yellow eyes puffed out of a swollen green spherical head, its mouth a dark jagged slash and its body misshapen. Spines or quills covered it like a bloated puffer fish.

Besides this unusual deity was a large orange octopus with a garish green eye set with an alien square black pupil.

The painting depicted a group of people daubed with peculiar symbols standing in the spiral room. A golden-haired woman was knelt before what looked like the oyster bowl. Blood flowed freely from her throat, but beside her on the other side of the font stood a man urinating into the vessel.

Josh rapidly described these things to Cuthbert, the words coming out as overexcited, half-gibberish.

Cuthbert's eyes glazed over, the electronic larynx once again discarded on the floor in favour of the black conch. "It's true," he croaked. "The Monophyletic Clade."

"What?" Josh said, straining to hear the man's devastated voice.

Josh and Nancy reached down to help Cuthbert as he tried to stand up. Josh bent back down and handed him the electric larynx but Cuthbert turned away from him, hiding the conch shell from view protectively.

Josh held the fake larynx and glanced nervously at Nancy.

Cuthbert slowly brought the shell up to his lips and blew.

Hunching, Cuthbert's face froze in a rictus from the effort he put into blowing into the conch, his cheeks red and expanding, veins bulging on his forehead.

Josh stepped forward, frightened that the old man was going to cause himself an injury – then the noise came. It began like a faraway foghorn and brought with it images of a rough angry sea on a stormy night. An icy pit spread throughout Josh's stomach. Nancy grabbed hold of his arm and he knew she felt it too: the cold.

The mournful wail heightened into a banshee scream that threatened the fabric of the listeners' eardrums.

Nancy clapped her hands over her ears; Josh was about to when he heard the screaming come from behind him.

David ran towards him from the spiral room, his face white with terror.

As Josh ran to his son's aid he could see Dylan's feet dancing some crazy jitterbug in the centre of the spiral. He was clearly having some kind of fit. There was no history of epilepsy in their family but that was exactly what this looked like. Josh fell to the floor and pinned Dylan's thrashing arms down. He didn't know what to do but knew that he needed to try and prevent further injury. He screamed for Nancy, and the sudden end of the conch's call made his voice fill the caverns.

Dylan's tongue protruded from his mouth and his face began to darken, vessels in the whites of his eyes bursting as his cheeks puffed out. He was choking. Josh grabbed him by the shoulders and recoiled as he felt the boy's body swell beneath his fingers. If this was some sort of allergic reaction to something it could be more dangerous than he had first thought.

"Nancy!" he shrieked, as Dylan spewed forth a torrent of orange slush.

His complexion began to change, the pigmentation of his oxygen-starved cheeks taking on a sickly green hue as the skin swelled and tightened. Josh pulled at his son's t-shirt but saw the reaction spread to his chest. The green pallor now covered all exposed skin, and his clothes split along the seams as his body mutated.

Dylan's death cries perforated Josh's eardrum. He reeled backwards and watched helplessly as his firstborn exploded into something large and green. Dylan's eyes glazed over with a thin yellow membrane, his nose sinking into his face as deep bloodless lacerations opened at either side of his throat.

A hissing sound made Josh turn from the green mess of his son to where water was bubbling freely from the oyster bowl. The barely-humanoid shape of Dylan staggered towards him like a combination of vegetable and zombie. His skin glistened with translucent excretion.

"The Tetraodonti."

Josh turned around and saw Cuthbert standing next to his wife and David.

"The Tetraodonti," Cuthbert repeated, his rasping barely audible over the strangulated gurgling of the thing that had once been Dylan.

"What the hell has happened to my son? What's that shit on him?" Nancy bellowed ferociously.

The little old man flinched and clutched the conch shell in his hands, still protective of his treasure. Cuthbert stepped forward and snatched the electric larynx off the floor where Josh had discarded it. "Your son," Cuthbert said, pointing the device at Dylan "has begun the ritual of Akkorokamui."

Josh backed away from Dylan, sloshing through the water that was beginning to pool within the spiral. If he hadn't witnessed the transformation himself he would have thought it some kind of expensive prosthetics. His son was the fucking creature from the Black Lagoon.

Dylan's new eyes bulged out from his recently-completed face. His rubbery green lips opened and closed aimlessly. The same thick orange stuff flowed from his mouth, and Josh saw it was comprised of minute balls, like caviar.

"Dyl..." Josh began, smiling, hoping that there was something of his son inside the putrid thing blocking their only exit. "Come on, stop pissing about now. We'll go to McDonalds."

Nancy groaned with the realisation that her husband's sanity had finally left him.

The Dylan-fish-man's jaw dropped, displaying teeth like green glass shards, and gave an unearthly, almost bird-like caw. A torrent of the orange stuff mixed with blood burst from his gullet and over his father. At the end of his cacophonic eruption his whole being inflated and dozens of foot-long spikes jutted out of his body.

"It has begun," Cuthbert said. He grabbed Nancy by the arm and spun her towards the green-skinned monster. As he let go of her, he dragged the conch shell across her throat.

Nancy fell into Josh's arms, blood spurting from her torn neck. He yelled her name as the life went out of her, her expression still one of confusion. She slumped onto the spiral mosaic, her blood mingling with what looked like urine.

Josh attempted to stem the flow of blood by pushing his hands against the wound but the slash was ragged and messy. Nancy's hot claret bubbled up between his fingers and she lay still.

Josh hurled himself at Cuthbert and, with one blow, knocked the old man off his feet. David rushed to his father's side and together they turned and headed towards the rising steps.

Dylan, or the thing that Cuthbert had called Tetraodonti, filled the narrow passage leading to the steps. An oozing yellow substance leaked from the creature's numerous spines, and it didn't take Josh long to guess that they were probably poisonous. It gave off its strange cry and ceased the discharge of the lumpy orange slush. The stuff mixed into the rising seawater that spewed endlessly from the oyster bowl.

Cuthbert sat up, just as the water was about to cover his head. Josh watched as his dead wife was submerged.

"Look," Cuthbert said, ignoring the blood seeping from a swollen split lip.

Josh had no choice other than to back up towards the tour guide.

The orange gunk in the water began to swirl and move, as though sentient. It churned and sunk through the seawater into the shells of the great spiral. Something began to manifest at the centre of the spiral and the whole mosaic was animated beneath the water.

"What is it?" Josh said, without taking his eyes from the orange whirlpool.

"The Tetraodonti births the Cephalopod," Cuthbert said, spellbound by what they were witnessing.

The word was familiar to Josh but his mind was too addled to know why.

A bulbous orange sphere ballooned from the water, a dark slit across its centre.

Josh thought back to the painting. It was an octopus – a huge orange octopus. It rose to the surface, its long tentacles snaking through the water, and opened its hideous cyclopean eye.

"What happens now?" Josh said, never letting go of David's hand.

"Together the Tetraodonti and the Cephalopod must become one, The Monophyletic Clade, and they will prepare the feast for the rising of Akkorokamui." Cuthbert waded through the waters towards the octopus. "I give myself freely," he said, throwing the electric larynx into the water and raising his arms before the Cephalopod.

Josh didn't know whether the old man was trying to buy them time or not, but as the thing that was once his son met Cuthbert and wrapped its slimy arms around him,

Josh knew they had a chance to escape. He moved quickly through the waist-high water, half-dragging David beside him. As they went past the writhing mass, Josh saw the Tetraodonti pull Cuthbert into its venom-spiked embrace.

The octopus wrapped the floating corpse of Nancy in its tentacles and joined Cuthbert and the green gill-man, smothering them with its sheer size and gelatinous bulk.

Josh pushed David towards the stone steps and they left the cavern.

Other than the noise of rushing water below, the only other sounds they could hear were one another's breathing.

As they burst out of the cupboard beneath the stairs and into the three-storey house above, Cuthbert's meaningless words replayed in his head: "Together the Tetraodonti and the Cephalopod must become one, The Monophyletic Clade, and they will prepare the feast for the rising of Akkorokamui."

Josh knew that they had awoken something old, something monstrous, and a vision of a continent-sized squid beneath the ocean floor seared through his head like a gunshot. Gigantic tentacles reaching across the world and flexing for the first time in millennia.

Josh stumbled along the hallway, following David through the open front door. The boy's legs give out below him at the same time as Josh felt his own collapse. Numbness spread from his waist down. He rolled onto his side on the rainy patio.

David looked on, frightened, immobilised, his arms pinned to his sides. "Dad," he managed to mewl as he screwed his eyes up in pain. Josh could only watch. Everything else was paralysed as David's skin turned iron-grey and begin to segment into thick curved scales.

A wave of seawater rushed out of the front door, washing them from the small garden and onto the pavement against their car. Josh felt the cold seep through him and took one last look at David. Thrashing about in the gutter by the kerb was a five-foot-long fish that had been his youngest child.

Another, bigger burst of water came from the house, completely obliterating the front of the building and coursing down the street. Josh felt the sudden electricity of sensation returning and realised he had changed too. Ahead, beneath the surface, he saw David swimming. His son turned his mutated, lipless face towards Josh, and Josh swam after him.

All around the world, people were metamorphosing as the necessary preparation for the feast of Akkorokamui had begun.

Matthew's Afterword

"I've been a friend of Jonathan's for two or three years now. We've a lot in common and our tastes are similar – except he tastes more 'yuck'. I knew from a short time after Jonathan opened his ever-flapping maw that his father, Les Butcher, (whom I secretly and hilariously refer to as 'the French Butcher') creates mind-knottingly spectacular optical illusionary art pieces. Jon propositioned me in a dimly lit bar with an offer I couldn't refuse, and I agreed to publishing an anthology where some authors he bandied together wrote stories inspired by The French Butcher's artwork. When I saw my piece of art I saw a colossal manta ray God buried under an inverted pyramid beneath the seabed. I kinda went from there onwards."

THE AUTHORS

Paula D. Ashe

Paula D. Ashe is a native Ohioan who lives in Indiana with her wife, their son, and too many pets. Her supernatural novella "Mater Nihil", was published by JWK Fiction in the *Four Ghosts* anthology in 2013. Her award winning short fiction has been published in several anthologies. Most recently her work has appeared in the heavy metal horror collection, *Axes of Evil II (2015)*, the third instalment of the Horror World Press series, *Eulogies III (2015)*, and Trevor Kennedy's Phantasmagoria Present's *Gruesome Grotesques Vol. 1*. Her short stories "The Mother of All Monsters" and "Carry On, Carrion" were both recognized with honourable mentions in Ellen Datlow's *Best Horror of the Year Volumes 7 and 8*. She is an irregular contributor to the Ladies of Horror flash fiction project, compiled and edited by Nina D'Arcangela. Paula is also one of seven contributing writers to *7 Magpies*, the first horror film anthology written and directed by African American women. She is completing a PhD in American Studies from Purdue University, for reasons unknown.

Duncan P. Bradshaw

In a large lidless saucepan, apply one Duncan P. Bradshaw under a moderate flame. Add three fistings of weirdness, a half dousing of mama's special sauce, complete with the alien gunk you found when you were sanding the skirting boards, and finally a dash of sarcastic mouse whiskers. The key thing is to ignore anything other than this method, which is to rotate the saucepan counter-clockwise until you notice the distinct smell of vulcanised steel hitting the back of your left nostril. Then, you sieve through the larger of your two Hadron Colliders and serve immediately, ideally with farm-reared punctuation paste and a firm handshake. For more recipes from this silly-billy, head to http://duncanpbradshaw.co.uk or if you want to run the risk of him collecting and selling your data to Farmville, then shoot over to https://www.facebook.com/duncanpbradshaw As he always says, 'Why don't you just sod off?' That cheeky scamp.

Jonathan Butcher.

Jonathan Butcher is the weirdo responsible for *The Chocolateman, What Good Girls Do, Demon Thingy*, and writing and starring in the short film *Stuck*. He's lived all over the UK, had some fun going Down Under, and even taught English to hundreds of squealing knee-high monsters in South Korea. He's currently living just outside of Brum, working on a novel about political and religious extremism, and excitedly awaiting the release of his first full-lengther this year, the gangland horror novel *The Children at the Bottom of the Gardden*.

Find me here: www.facebook.com/jonathanbutcherauthor

Les Butcher

Well, here I am at last in print, and not on a police constable's note pad!! I am so chuffed that at my age after getting writer's cramp so many times, my efforts have hopefully been recognized.

My designing goes back about 60 years and I don't have a clue as to why I started; glad I did though. I have sold some for a pittance on occasion, but my main reward is in the execution of them.

I was born and bred in Peckham, South East London – good old Del Boy land – way back in 1940. My mum brought up my late sister and myself as my father didn't bother to come back after his army service. Therefore we didn't have much income, but my lovely mum did a great job on us both.

After primary school days I went to grammar school, but the London accent remained. I was good at essays even then in those days. Fame has taken a bleedin' long time to find me.

At the age of nearly 40 I and my wife moved here to Newquay in Cornwall and here our son was born. He has been the apple of our eyes ever since. Here is written proof of what a great feller and love of our lives that he is. The effort that he has put in to this book is amazing and I thank him so much.

I hope that it is successful for all concerned.

P.S. Anybody want to buy some designs cheap? Get in touch with Jonathan via jonathan.btchr@gmail.com!

Matthew Cash.

Matthew Cash, or Matty-Bob Cash as he is known to most, was born and raised in Suffolk; which is the setting for his debut novel Pinprick. He is compiler and editor of Death By Chocolate, a chocoholic horror Anthology, Sparks, the 12Days: STOCKING FILLERS Anthology, and its subsequent yearly annuals and has numerous releases on Kindle and several collections in paperback.

In 2016 he started his own label Burdizzo Books, with the intention of compiling and releasing charity anthologies a few times a year. He is currently working on numerous projects, his second novel FUR will hopefully be launched 2018.

He has always written stories since he first learnt to write and most, although not all, tend to slip into the many layered murky depths of the Horror genre.

His influences ranged from when he first started reading to Present day are, to name but a small select few; Roald Dahl, James Herbert, Clive Barker, Stephen King, Stephen Laws, and more recently he enjoys Adam Nevill, F.R Tallis, Michael Bray, Gary Fry, William Meikle and Iain Rob Wright (who featured Matty-Bob in his famous A-Z of Horror title M is For Matty-Bob, plus Matthew wrote his own version of events which was included as a bonus).

He is a father of two, a husband of one and a zoo keeper of numerous fur babies.

You can find him here:

www.facebook.com/pinprickbymatthewcash

https://www.amazon.co.uk/-/e/B010MQTWKK

J.G. Clay

J.G. Clay is a British author, currently residing in the heart of England. Unleashing his unique combination of cosmic horror, dark fiction and science fiction with the first volume of 'The Tales of Blood And Sulphur' in 2015, Clay will be casting his beady eye on Hell, alternative Earths and England's second city in forthcoming works. He promises an endless supply of 'Nightmare Fuel For The Modern Age'.

Away from the printed page, J.G is a bass playing, Birmingham City supporting family man with a fondness for real ale and the Baggie/Britpop era of British Music.

Links

Website: www.jgclayhorror.com

Facebook: https://www.facebook.com/jgclay1973

Twitter: https://twitter.com/JGClay1

David Court

David Court is a short story author and novelist, whose works have appeared in over a dozen venues including Tales to Terrify, Strangely Funny, Fears Accomplice and The Voices Within. Whilst primarily a horror writer, he also writes science fiction, poetry and satire.

His writing style has been described as "Darkly cynical" and "Quirky and highly readable" and David can't bring himself to disagree with either of those statements.

Growing up in the UK in the eighties, David's earliest influences were the books of Stephen King and Clive Barker, and the films of John Carpenter and George Romero. The first wave of Video Nasties may also have had a profound effect on his psyche.

As well as writing for Stitched Smile Publications, David works as a Software Developer and lives in Coventry with his wife, three cats and an ever-growing beard. David's wife once asked him if he'd write about how great she was. David replied that he would, because he specialized in short fiction. Despite that, they are still married.

Em Dehaney

Em Dehaney is a mother of two, a writer of fantasy and a drinker of tea.

By night she is The Black Nun, editor and whip-cracker at Burdizzo Books.

By day you can always find her at

http://www.emdehaney.com/

or lurking about on Facebook posting pictures of witches

https://www.facebook.com/emdehaney/

You can also follow Em on Twitter @emdehaney

Her debut short fiction collection Food Of The Gods is available now on Amazon:

Kayleigh Marie Edwards

Kayleigh Marie Edwards is from a town in South Wales where nothing ever happens and a lot of people only wear tracksuits. She lives alone in a house full of horror merchandise and a cat that has recently learned how to tip over furniture. She's a pretty big fan of the whole cheese scene. She has two younger siblings who couldn't be more different, and yet are equally amusing in entirely separate ways. You might think that none of this information is relevant to her writing. But you'd be wrong.

Lydian Faust

Lydian Faust is a writer of horror and dark fiction. She is also a painter who likes to lay it on thick. Ms. Faust lives in one of the murder capitals of the United States of America. Her hobbies include nachos and alien conspiracy theories.

You can find her at www.lydianfaust.com, on Facebook at www.facebook.com/lydianfaust, and on Twitter

@LydianFaust.

Adam Millard

Adam Millard is the author of twenty-six novels, thirteen novellas, and more than two hundred short stories, which can be found in various collections, magazine, and anthologies. Probably best known for his post-apocalyptic fiction, Adam also writes fantasy/horror for children and Bizarro fiction for several publishers. His work has recently been translated for the German market.

www.adammillard.co.uk

John McNee

John McNee is the writer of numerous strange and disturbing horror stories, published in a variety of strange and disturbing anthologies, as well as the novel 'Prince of Nightmares'.

He is also the creator of Grudgehaven and the author of 'Grudge Punk', a collection of short stories detailing the lives and deaths of its gruesome inhabitants.

He lives in Glasgow and can easily be sought out on Facebook, Goodreads, Twitter and at his website,

www.johnmcnee.com.

Kit Power

Kit Power lives in Milton Keynes and writes horror and dark crime fiction, with occasional forays into dystopian science fiction. He has a novel, 'GodBomb!', and a novella collection 'Breaking Point' - both available on Kindle and in paperback and published by The Sinister Horror Company - and his debut short fiction and essay collection, the snappily titled 'A Warning About Your Future Enslavement That You WIll DIsmiss As A Collection Of Short Fiction And Essays By Kit Power' is also available in Kindle ebook and regular paperback worldwide.

In his increasingly inaccurately labelled spare time, he podcasts - on his own show, Watching Robocop With Kit Power, and as one quarter of the legendary Wrong With Authority team.

For weekly early access to his fiction, non-fiction, and podcasting work, visit www.patreon.com/kitpower .

He also regularly blogs for Gingernuts of Horror, Europe's most popular independent review site.

P.S....

If you would like a print of any of the designs in this book, or would like to see more of the collection, or would even like a personalised piece designed for you or someone you know, pop a quick email to jonathan.btchr@gmail.com

COMING SOON FROM BURDIZZO BOOKS

THE CHILDREN AT THE BOTTOM OF THE GARDDEN

JONATHAN BUTCHER

At the edge of the coastal city of Seadon there stands a dilapidated farmhouse, and at the back of the farmhouse there is a crowd of rotten trees, where something titters and calls.

The Gardden.

Its playful voice promises games, magic, wonders, lies – and roaring torrents of blood.

It speaks not just to its eccentric keeper, Thomas, but also to the outcasts and deviants from Seadon's criminal underworld.

At first they are too distracted by their own tangled mistakes and violent lives to notice, but one by one they'll come: a restless Goth, a cheating waster, a sullen concubine, a perverted drug baron, and a murderous sociopath.

Haunted by shadowed things with coal-black eyes, something malicious and ancient will lure them ever closer. And on a summer's day not long from now, they'll gather beneath the leaves in a place where nightmares become flesh, secrets rise up from the dark, and a voice coaxes them to play and stay, yes yes yes, forever.

Printed in Great Britain
by Amazon